Midnight Encounter

by
Glenna Finley

... I have nightly since
Dreamt of encounters 'twixt
thyself and me.
Coriolanus, Shakespeare

A SIGNET BOOK

NEW AMERICAN LIBRARY

TIMES MIRROR

PUBLISHER'S NOTE

This novel is a work of fiction. Names, characters, places, and incidents are either the product of the author's imagination or are used fictitiously, and any resemblance to actual persons, living or dead, events, or locales is entirely coincidental.

NAL BOOKS ARE AVAILABLE AT QUANTITY DISCOUNTS WHEN USED TO PROMOTE PRODUCTS OR SERVICES FOR INFORMATION PLEASE WRITE TO PREMIUM MARKETING DIVISION, THE NEW AMERICAN LIBRARY, INC., 1633 BROADWAY, NEW YORK, NEW YORK 10019.

SIGNET TRADEMARK REG. U.S. PAT. OFF. AND FOREIGN COUNTRIES
REGISTERED TRADEMARK—MARCA REGISTRADA
HECHO EN CHICAGO, U.S.A.

SIGNET, SIGNET CLASSICS, MENTOR, PLUME, MERIDIAN AND NAL BOOKS are published by The New American Library, Inc., 1633 Broadway, New York, New York 10019

First Printing, March, 1981

1 2 3 4 5 6 7 8 9

PRINTED IN THE UNITED STATES OF AMERICA

Chapter One

"You must be out of your mind," Adam Driscoll told his sister on a long-distance phone call. "What in the devil makes you think I have time to entertain your roommate here in New Orleans? *She's* the one on vacation—I'm still working."

An undignified snort from the other end of the wire showed what Nora Driscoll thought of that pronouncement. "I've seen you at work before," she told him. "It won't hurt you to fit in Toni instead of that brunette you were spending your money on when I saw you last week. I should think that an economic consultant would choose a lunch date with a little more intellect and a little less cleavage."

"I don't know why you're complaining," he replied dryly. "I liked the proportions just the way they were."

"That was obvious. You weren't the only man impressed. The waiter filled her water glass eight times during lunch. I counted."

"I doubt if the *Guinness Book of Records* would be interested and frankly I don't think it's worth a long-distance call myself. Next time concentrate on your filet of sole and I'll manage the rest."

"I just mentioned it. I don't see why you object

1

to taking Toni out. There's certainly nothing wrong with her measurements. Maybe she couldn't compete with that brunette in some places . . ."

"Would you mind dropping the brunette?" Adam interrupted, starting to sound annoyed.

"Not at all. I hope you will, too. You'd never get ahead with that kind of woman. Imagine introducing her to the head of the firm."

"Since she's the niece of one of the directors, an introduction wouldn't be necessary. She's also a tax lawyer which shows what you know about first impressions. May I suggest that you avoid any more editorial comments until you manage to drag Mike to the altar next month. That way your intended won't find out what a pinhead he's acquiring."

"I'll keep your suggestion in mind," his sister replied calmly. "Now can we get back to Toni?"

"If you insist. But I wasn't kidding about being busy for the next few days."

"You aren't *that* busy, Adam. Besides, she knows you're in New Orleans."

"I don't see how."

"I told her, that's how. She called a few minutes ago about some mail that she wanted forwarded and I just happened to mention that you were spending the weekend in New Orleans, too."

"I don't imagine that she was thrilled to hear it," Adam said dourly. "She's probably already checked out of her hotel to play it safe."

"She doesn't even suspect that you might call and I didn't let on. It would be awful if you stood her up twice."

"I *told* you that damned meeting of mine ran overtime. When I tried to call Toni later there wasn't any answer." He went on defensively, "I had to eat someplace afterward. It was just rotten luck that I ran into her at that restaurant."

"Especially since you were with a redhead at the time."

"She's a friend of mine and she was eating alone because she'd taken her husband to the airport—" Adam broke off angrily. "Dammit, I'm sick of explaining! One missed date a month ago and your roommate has been handing me a frozen mitt ever since—"

"Exactly," his sister interjected triumphantly. "But since she's my maid of honor and you'll be best man at my wedding, it's up to you to put things right."

"Oh, hell! I suppose I can try."

"Well, don't make it sound like such a sacrifice. She's a wonderful person and she certainly doesn't have to beat the bushes for a dinner date. Not with her figure and profile."

"You make it sound as if that's all men care about," Adam felt bound to protest.

Nora ignored his retort, continuing with her orders. "Maybe you can talk your way back into Toni's good graces one way or another. You're usually pretty lucky at that." She kept her words offhand since she had no intention of strewing any compliments in her brother's path.

In Nora's opinion—it would have been gilding the lily. For the past ten years, plenty of women had reassured Adam about his physical attraction. It wasn't surprising, since he was a rangy six-footer with broad shoulders that tapered to a lean waist and hips. His thick fair hair had a tendency to fall over his forehead at times but, even then, he presented an assured appearance that made his business competitors tread lightly. At age thirty, he made no assertions that his bachelorhood was to be a permanent state and, as a consequence, most women he dated tried their darnedest to change his lifestyle. Adam wisely did nothing to discourage their efforts.

Naturally his sister was convinced that such an existence would ruin any man; Adam should suffer a little like everybody else.

The germ of an idea evolved in Nora's mind after Toni had coldly rebuffed Adam's apologies for the broken date—at last showing him that he couldn't pull a *faux pas* without suffering some consequences. Adam couldn't completely ignore Toni after that either, because, as his sister's roommate, she was still on the fringes of his life. Later, when Toni found she had some vacation time coming in March, Nora suggested New Orleans and remained discreetly silent about Adam's impending business trip to the same place.

Her maneuvering succeeded beyond belief. Both Adam and Toni were on the same territory, in the same hotel, and, if phone conversations were to be believed, more than a little bored. All she had to do was give them a verbal shove.

She crossed her fingers and grinned as she heard Adam reluctantly say, "Well, I can give her a ring. If she hangs up on me, that's the end of it. Even for the sake of your wedding—one phone call's as far as I go."

"She won't hang up on you."

"What makes you so sure?"

Nora was tempted to say, "because I told her not

to," but prudently decided against it—knowing that Adam could be pushed only so far. "Toni isn't silly enough to hold a grudge. She's been a little annoyed at you but that's in the past."

"Okay. If having dinner will smooth her ruffled feelings, I'll go along with the game. But just this once. Nora. From now on, you concentrate on telling that fiancé of yours what to do and leave me alone. Where's Toni staying here in New Orleans?"

"Well, actually she's in the same place as you are." His sister heard his quick intake of breath and hurried on. "It's just a coincidence. She asked me about New Orleans hotels long before I knew you were going to be down there."

"All right. Relax. I'm just glad I heard about it before I ran into her in the lobby."

"Or in the dining room when you were with another woman."

"Good-bye, Nora." His tone was abruptly dismissive.

"Adam—you be nice to her."

"Good Lord, you make it sound as if I spend my time beating women. I'll phone and invite her out to dinner. The rest is up to her." He put down the receiver then before Nora could add any other instructions.

If the truth had been told, Adam wasn't as reluctant to make the phone call as he pretended. New Orleans wasn't the kind of town for a cloistered life. He'd spent the day in business conferences and he'd welcomed the relaxing solitude of his hotel room when he'd first walked in, but the feeling had quickly passed. Besides, his dealings with Toni Morgan had been so brief that they had merely whetted his appetite. It was an indulgence, because he seldom permitted his social life to encroach on his sister's acquaintances. Nora had a lamentable tendency to stand on the sidelines and direct even though she was three years younger. Not that getting involved was a real problem as far as Toni was concerned. He'd shared a few cups of coffee with her when she'd first moved in with Nora. Then he'd managed to stand her up on their first dinner date and gotten caught wining and dining another woman a few hours later. After that, his conversations with Toni had stopped abruptly—either on the telephone or when he'd dropped in at the apartment.

Adam had been more annoyed by her attitude than he'd let on to Nora. For one thing, Antonia Morgan was an extremely attractive young woman, with the kind of shiny brown hair that Adam liked and a pair of dark blue eyes that were hard to forget. When he'd first met her, those blue eyes were warm and inviting, framed by thick lashes that dropped in confusion whenever he'd teased her about her dedication to her job. She headed a demonstration kitchen for an advertising agency that specialized in food accounts and she had a weakness for baking chocolate-chip cookies on weekends. As far as Adam was concerned, this made her a pearl beyond price but Nora swore that she'd had to move her wedding date forward to be sure of being able to fit into her bridal gown when the time came.

Adam stared at the phone receiver speculatively before he picked it up again. With any luck, Toni might have brought some of those chocolate-chip cookies with her. As a visitor to New Orleans, he should indulge in pralines or *beignets* at the French

Market, but for his money, they weren't in the same class.

The hotel operator put through his call promptly, but the phone rang without response. Adam's thoughts of a pleasant dinner with Toni being suitably grateful for his company suddenly dimmed and he frowned. He'd let it ring two more times and then to hell with the whole affair! Nora couldn't complain and as far as the elusive Toni went—

"What is it?" Her response came abruptly as he'd just started to put down the receiver. She didn't sound any more inviting when she said, "Oh, damn! Why didn't I just let it ring?"

"Wait! Don't hang up," he commanded.

"Who *is* this?" Her voice was coldly suspicious.

"Adam."

"Who?"

"A for abysmal, D for delayed, another A for—"

"Almighty?" she cut in. "And M for 'Meet me later.'"

"I thought you'd remember," he said dryly.

"Well, Nora said you were in town. She didn't say that I couldn't take a bath in the meantime."

"You mean . . ."

"I mean that I'm dripping over the rug and the phone's under the air conditioner. So, if you don't mind, I'll hang up. Give my best to Nora when you see her."

His vision of undraped femininity that her first words had evoked was shattered rudely by her final utterance. Adam spoke hastily, before her receiver could go down. "Wait a minute—this won't take long—"

"That's good—oh, damn!"

The last words were accompanied by a distinct thud. Adam frowned and said, "Toni? Are you still there?"

There was a muffled comment, then she managed, "I'm here—but I'm not sure about the phone. I dropped it when my towel slipped."

"Did you get it back?"

"The towel or the phone?"

Adam chose not to answer that one. "I won't keep you," he replied instead. "Nora said you might be free for dinner with me. Is that right?"

"But how did she know?"

Adam didn't give her time to think about it. "We can eat here in the hotel or go down the street. Shall I meet you in the lobby in—say a half hour?"

"Well—" Her indecision was punctuated by a sneeze.

"You'd better finish with a hot shower," Adam said briskly. "If that doesn't do the trick—you can have a hot toddy before dinner. I'll meet you in the lobby in a half hour."

He hesitated for the barest interval before dropping his receiver back on the hook. Then he grinned triumphantly at it. Toni's acceptance was hardly enthusiastic but it would be some time before she could compare notes with Nora and find that she'd been shanghaied into accepting. By then, it would be too late to matter.

Three floors above him, Toni pulled the towel around her and headed back to the bathroom, wondering why she'd let Adam Driscoll talk her into a dinner date after the way he'd acted before. She dropped the towel on a hamper and stepped back into the soothing warmth of the bubble bath she'd abandoned.

Submerging to her chin, she reached for her washcloth and absently started to soap it. The truth was, she'd found it hard to whip up righteous indignation when Adam had called.

Her solitary vacation, which had sounded so appealing when planned, was turning out to be a damp squib. Not that she wanted to be back at work instead. Sometimes she thought that if she had to figure out one more way to incorporate brewer's yeast or wheat germ in a recipe she'd run screaming for the roof. Which was absurd, she told herself, soaping vigorously. She earned an excellent salary, and was surrounded by intelligent people. It was a little tiresome that most of her lunch dates were at the health-food restaurant in the next block but it was convenient so it could only be expected. Somehow, that's why New Orleans had sounded so appealing. In all the restaurants she'd read about, there hadn't been one mention of soy cakes, carob candy, or braised celery. But even a double portion of greasy *beignets* saturated with powdered sugar on her first two mornings in the French Quarter had only lifted her spirits momentarily.

'She stood up and turned on the shower to rinse off the bubble bath, afterward giving her reflection a wry appraisal as she reached for a dry towel. Might as well face it, she told herself. Solitary vacations were simply not what travel writers avowed. And that was the only reason she'd accepted Adam's dinner invitation.

She caught another glimpse of herself in the steamy mirror as she replaced the towel and wrinkled her nose derisively. If she'd just wanted company for the evening, her heartbeat wouldn't be thudding along at double time.

Not that she had the slightest intention of letting Adam know her reaction. The two of them would have a nice, civilized but innocuous dinner. If the conversation flagged, they could always discuss the forthcoming wedding. Afterward, she could say that she was expecting a phone call as an excuse to cut the evening short.

She donned clean underthings, and padded out to the closet to take a pale-yellow silk dress with a slim skirt off the hanger. Thank heavens, she'd put it in her suitcase at the last minute among her more practical travel outfits. Her brown blazer could serve as a topcoat since the March climate in New Orleans was almost lamblike. During the day, the wind still held touches of frost but when it died down, the weather showed a deep southern balm.

She ran a brush over her brown hair, happy that her last cut had left it an easy-to-manage collar length. A touch of shadow emphasized and deepened the blue of her eyes, and she used soft red lipstick sparingly to complete her makeup. She remembered all too vividly the beautiful grooming of the redhead that Adam had escorted on that fateful night. That was the only reason she was taking so much trouble, she told herself and then muttered, "Liar," at her face in the mirror.

A moment later, she picked up her purse and blazer, checked to make sure she had her room key, and then headed for the elevator.

Adam, wearing a dark blue blazer and charcoal slacks, was surveying a window display of luggage in a nearby gift shop as she got out in the lobby. Toni hesitated, impressed again by his blatant masculinity.

His tall figure gave an impression of straight, hard lines where assurance and self-discipline dominated. If there was any softness in his nature, it was well hidden. Certainly it wasn't visible in that level gray-eyed glance or around his stern mouth and the firm set of his jaw. Toni had thought the first time she'd seen him that he was far from the impetuous type. Yet when he turned to behold her, there was devilment in his deliberate appraisal and she had a niggling feeling that somehow she'd pegged him wrong.

He walked across to meet her. "Right on time," he said approvingly.

"You sound surprised."

"Not at all. Nora mentioned that promptness was one of your virtues. The subject came up after she kept me waiting for a half hour on a street corner and I objected." When Toni remained pointedly silent, a wave of red swept up his tanned cheeks. "Hell! I forgot about doing the same thing to you." He scowled suddenly. "I don't mean that I forgot it—dammit, I just ..."

". . . wasn't going to mention it," she supplied helpfully, delighted that his customary assurance had deserted him.

"You're right. I wasn't going to mention that or the fact that I dragged you out of the bath. At least you don't appear to have suffered from *that*," he added with a glance that was remarkably thorough.

Toni felt a wave of elation. Things were definitely going better than she'd hoped. "I've survived fine, thanks."

Adam's grin was rueful. "Then this is where I change the subject and ask if you'd like to stay here in the French Quarter to eat?"

"Anything sounds good to me." Toni had no intention of admitting that if he hadn't called she would have settled for a sandwich in the nearest coffee shop.

"There's Brennan's. It's just a block away on Royal Street." He moved her closer to the gift shop so a bellman could wheel a towering load of luggage past them. "Or we can eat here in the hotel if we don't get flattened by the traffic first." The last was added when a convention group emerged from a meeting room and headed en masse for the elevators.

"Brennan's will be great. I've read about it and always wanted to eat there." Toni held out her blazer and let him help her into it before they went down some wide marble steps to the street. Once outside, Adam declined the doorman's offer of a cab and shook his head when the driver of a decorated horse cart offered to take them on a tour of the Quarter.

Adam took a deep breath when they finally reached an uncrowded part of sidewalk and headed toward Royal Street. "Nobody in New Orleans misses a bet when it comes to tourists. Of course, that's what you expect if your hotel's in the French Quarter."

"I'm finding that out," Toni acknowledged. "It was nice of Nora to recommend it, though. I didn't know where to stay." Her voice trailed off as suspicion surfaced. "Do you stay at this hotel every time you come to town?"

"Not always," Adam prevaricated. "But it's a good one and handy to most of the well-known restaurants. Have you been to Bourbon Street yet?"

"I walked there this morning on the way to the center of town. There wasn't anything unusual about it. To be honest, I was a little disappointed."

"That's because it doesn't really get rolling until

after dark." Adam suddenly recalled some of the displays the last time he'd seen Bourbon Street and decided on a different tack. "I doubt if you'd be interested. There are lots of other places in town to hear jazz or see the nightclub offerings."

Toni knew that jazz was a minor attraction of Bourbon Street but she didn't argue. Especially as they'd just pulled up outside Brennan's display window which featured a big dinner menu.

"Maybe you'd better take a look and see if there's anything that appeals to you," Adam suggested. "There's always a salad but I'm not sure about their vegetarian menu . . ."

"What in the dickens has Nora been telling you?"

He looked blank. "Nothing, except that you work with food clients at that kitchen of yours. Something about recipes and developing nutritional trends, isn't it?"

"That doesn't mean that I eat blackstrap molasses twenty-four hours a day. Especially when I'm on vacation in New Orleans," she told him. "This morning I bought pralines in the French Market and later I had a chocolate soda for lunch. I think a reaction is setting in."

"Good. That's when I like to come on the scene. When a woman's weak and willing," Adam said, grinning. "Let's go in and overdose on calories. Now I won't have to feel guilty if I have dessert."

If Toni hadn't extended an olive branch by then, she certainly would have a little later when they were seated at a table for two next to the inner palm court of the restaurant. After the formality of ordering was finished, she and Adam sat back to leisurely enjoy the feast that followed. There was a thick onion soup lavishly garnished with cheese plus a French bread topping. The green salad which came next was crisp and delicately flavored with a house dressing. Toni managed to feel virtuous about calories at that point but when the waiter appeared with their entree, she discarded logic and simply picked up her fork. The main course was a magnificent concoction of chicken breasts sautéed in lemon butter and served with artichoke bottoms plus fresh mushrooms. Considerably later, when it was time for dessert the waiter brought a strawberry mousse, and both Adam and Toni groaned in protest.

"I simply can't," Toni told him. "I'll have to be rolled out the front door as it is."

"This is very cold and slips down easily, madam," the waiter assured her, as he ladled generous portions in front of them, adding fresh strawberries as a topping.

"Mmmm—delicious!" Adam confirmed. "Try a taste at least, Toni."

After that there was no more conversation until they surveyed the empty plates in front of them and met each other's rueful glances.

"I don't see how you can visit New Orleans every six months and still fit into your clothes," Toni commented as she took a sip of strong coffee. "That had to be the finest dinner I've ever eaten."

Adam surveyed her with narrowed eyes. "I'm glad to see you've joined the human race with all its failings. After hearing Nora's accounts of your career—I wasn't quite sure what to expect."

Toni fiddled with the spoon on her saucer, keeping her gaze discreetly lowered as well. "Probably it was a Freudian slip all along."

"What are you talking about?"

"The reason you stood me up that other time. It was self-protection."

"I thought we were going to forget about that," he said somewhat grimly.

Her glance came up then, shining with laughter. "After such a splendid dinner, too."

"Never mind. I'll find a way to get my own back," Adam assured her as he reached for his wallet to settle the bill. The waiter was so solicitous in pouring more coffee that Toni could only conclude his tip was lavish as well. Eventually Adam put his napkin on the table and shoved back his chair. "How about strolling around a few blocks to counteract the calories? Or would you rather go straight back to the hotel?"

"A walk would be nice," she told him as she gathered up her purse and stood beside him. She waited until they were ushered to the restaurant foyer, past the genial maitre d', and on Royal Street again before asking, "Which way?"

"It doesn't matter." Adam looked down the sidewalk to his right after helping her on with her blazer jacket and then suddenly his fingers gripped her shoulders so strongly that she winced. "Damn! I'm sorry," he said. His grip relaxed but only for a moment. The next thing, he'd pulled her into a shadowed storefront next to the restaurant where the windows were filled with foreign coins, stamps, and displays of antique lead soldiers. "Look up!" he said commandingly, at the same time putting a strong arm around her so that she was forced to do just that. Then, without any further hesitation, he bent and covered her lips with his.

All Toni could do was stand motionless in his steel-like grip, but she was dazedly conscious that Adam's kiss showed every evidence of proficiency—cool, firm, and undeniably possessive. And while it was far more than just a salute, Toni discovered that he made no effort to part her lips as he pulled her even closer. If anything, he seemed intent on keeping her mouth closed.

When he finally raised his head, he confirmed her suspicion, saying brusquely, "Keep quiet—I'll explain later."

"You'll explain now." Toni's voice was subdued, but she made no attempt to hide her anger. "What's the idea of pouncing on me?"

"Relax—it was nothing personal," Adam said absently as he looked over his shoulder. "Those men on the sidewalk—I didn't want them to recognize me. Just concentrate on that shop window for a minute until I can tell whether the coast is clear."

Toni wasn't happy about his casual dismissal of her participation in that kiss but she shrugged off her anger and even managed to concentrate on the display window as he requested. "They're very nice," she said finally, trying to sound calmly matter-of-fact. When there was no response, she glanced around and saw that Adam had edged closer to the sidewalk, his attention still directed toward the end of the block. "I said they're very nice," she repeated.

"What's nice?" he asked, turning to face her.

"The toy soldiers." Her voice sharpened. "Why am I the only one looking at them?"

"Sorry." His stern features softened as he came to her side. "They *are* unique, aren't they? Not many women appreciate such things. There are some more shops of them down this way," he said, taking her elbow and moving her to the sidewalk. "We can do a circle tour and get that exercise we were talking about."

Toni risked a sideways glance at his profile. As window-shopping material, toy soldiers weren't too thrilling and Adam wasn't paying attention to anything except the crowds of strolling pedestrians ahead of them. When they came to a corner close to the hotel, he increased the pressure on her elbow, and turned her down St. Louis Street. The sidewalk strollers were even thicker there, watching groups of jazz musicians performing on street corners.

"Are we going to Bourbon Street?" Toni asked, thoroughly confused by then, yet caught up in the carnival atmosphere.

Adam didn't answer right away and when he did, Toni felt he hadn't welcomed her interruption. "We might as well. Bourbon Street's where the action is. Unless you'd rather go back to the hotel?"

From the way he spoke, she knew that she'd be sent on her way with a hasty good-bye if she even dithered. Somehow, he'd changed completely as soon as they'd left the restaurant. It wasn't that they were back to in-fighting or squabbling; instead, she was being pointedly ignored. Which was almost worse, she decided, and moved stubbornly closer as they headed toward Bourbon Street. "I'm enjoying it," she said blithely, as if she had Adam's attention. "Just look at that tap dancer. He can't be more than eight years old. I wonder if he's here every night. Probably that man passing the hat is his father."

As she suspected, Adam merely nodded and he didn't let her linger as they passed a trio which was providing accompaniment for the young dancer. Toni's frown deepened as she tried to discover what held Adam's attention. It certainly wasn't the horse-drawn carriage filled with tourists or the wrought-iron balconies which were seen throughout the French Quarter. And it surely wasn't the pushcart merchants that he was determinedly avoiding.

The old-fashioned street lights cast a flickering illumination down on the narrow, none-too-clean street as they walked along. Toni had already discovered that the broken concrete and potholes of the Quarter sidewalks could prove hazardous, and she was forced to watch her step. She had no intention of twisting her ankle just when things were getting interesting!

They passed some coffee bars and a famous restaurant where black-coated waiters on their break lounged at the delivery doors. Despite the crowded sidewalks and the throngs of street musicians, a sense of decorum prevailed but the atmosphere changed as soon as Adam led Toni around the corner into Bourbon Street.

Suddenly the pedestrians solidified into one solid block of humanity and Toni became caught up in the excitement.

Adam kept a firm grip on her arm and struggled to find a passage through the revelers. "Let's keep going."

She only half-heard his embarrassed mutter because by then her gaze had shifted to the scene which held the attention of the crowd—a gaudy go-go establishment across the street. The open doors made it impossible to miss the almost nude body of a woman on the stage, even without the mammoth reflecting mirrors which flanked her. A steady stream of jazz blared out and the voluptuous dancer who was wearing only a G-string and two strategically placed sequins didn't miss a beat of the music. The fact that she was entertaining half of Bourbon Street as well as the people in the tavern apparently didn't faze the management.

By then, Adam had hold of Toni's hand and pulled her out of range but she discovered the same atmosphere prevailed almost everywhere along the next few blocks. Bourbon Street bars and eating places that had been discreetly shuttered during the day were alive and swinging at night. Doors were propped wide open to give passersby a sampling of the feature inside. If that wasn't explicit enough, there were sidewalk barkers to entice the customers. Toni's cheeks carried a permanent flush during the first block even though she wasn't particularly surprised at the offerings. After the initial shock, it was more interesting to watch the crowds surging down the street. There were tourists who were wide-eyed at the expanse of flesh, others who stood sedately in front of a few famous French Quarter restaurants, interested in a different sampling, and finally the jazz devotees whose attention stayed strictly on the street musicians that were to be found on almost every corner.

"Damn! I didn't expect this. I should have sent you back to the hotel," Adam said, when they'd reached the third block of unfettered Bourbon hilarity.

"Oh, for heaven's sakes—I'm not about to faint on the sidewalk. There isn't room, for one thing." She stayed close to avoid a group of conventioneers who were trying to decide which establishment they wanted to patronize. Adam pulled her against him until the men had passed and then he urged her forward again. Toni was so inured to the flesh markets by then that her attention lingered on his set profile. "You don't look particularly thrilled," she remarked.

"It isn't what I'd have chosen."

His terse comment puzzled her even more. "Well, then—why don't we go back?"

She had barely gotten the words out when he said, "I wanted to check out somebody. But now, damned if I haven't lost sight of him."

The music and the carnival atmosphere faded into the background for a moment as Toni recognized the grim undertone in his voice. "What can I do to help?" she asked levelly.

"If you wouldn't mind being parked for the moment—I could make a quick search of the next block or so." He led her to a fairly deserted spot on the sidewalk in front of a shop specializing in soft sculpture. "You'll be okay here, I think. I'll be back within ten minutes. If anybody bothers you—"

"Nora and I took a session of judo," she informed him, amused by his worried look. "Go ahead. I'll just stand here and window-shop."

As Adam's tall form disappeared into the people clogging the street, Toni turned her attention to the display window behind her. She stared for a minute and then started to laugh helplessly. What they'd chosen as an ordinary gift shop featured an X-rated display of soft sculpture and pillows to lure sensation-seeking tourists. The sign above the merchandise promised easy mailing and Toni tried to picture Nora's face if she received one as a souvenir.

The next shop was another topless establishment and then there was a T-shirt emporium whose sample messages weren't the kind usually noted in department stores. Toni moved on again.

Fortunately there was a delicatessen on the next crowded corner and she was able to linger, buying a newspaper when a clerk materialized. She was back on the sidewalk again when she noticed a brightly lit room across the street where big windows revealed three women lounging in easy chairs. It looked like a hotel lobby except that the young women weren't overloaded with clothes. The fabric of their dresses was skimpy, the necklines were slashed to the navel, and the hemlines high. If there'd been any doubt as to the kind of establishment, it was resolved by red lights surrounding the main door and a young woman who leaned against it. She was shouting, "Come in, come in and take your choice. Ten dollars for thirty minutes or make a deal for longer. Hiya, honey— come on in. You can investigate the merchandise first-hand." The last was said to a man walking by.

Toni felt a touch on her own arm at that point and jumped a foot. "Thank God!" she said fervently, recognizing Adam. "I felt as if I'd been thrown away."

He shot a look at the red-light emporium across the street and nodded grimly. "A little of that goes a long way. Come on, let's go. We'll have a drink at the hotel."

"Yes, please," she murmured, falling into step beside him.

After that, they were both unnaturally silent as they threaded their way through the high-spirited visitors who, by then, created a solid stream of humanity along the pedestrian mall. Apparently Adam was unsuccessful at finding his quarry and Toni realized that it wasn't the time to discuss it. Her own feelings were a mixed bag but for a very different reason and it took her the few blocks back to the hotel before she'd sorted out her reactions to the Bourbon Street scene.

"Now I know," she muttered almost to herself as Adam ushered her through a side door which led to the hotel's elegant marble foyer.

"What are you talking about?"

"Bourbon Street. I was trying to think what surprised me most about all the go-go dancers and the women in that 'red light'—" She paused, trying to find a diplomatic term.

Adam didn't help her but his eyebrows went up.

"The place on the corner," she said undeterred. "Talk about a shabby tiger!"

His steps slowed. "I had a feeling that you were wishing you could sink into a crack in the sidewalk most of the time."

"Just at first. After that, I was noticing how bored those dancers looked. Didn't you see?" Looking up, she noted his amused expression. "Never mind," she went on hastily. "You don't have to explain that there wasn't anybody else in the place watching their faces."

"Such research does you credit. Shall we sit on one of those leather sofas in the back of the lobby bar? There are coffee and pastries if you'd prefer but frankly I want something tall and cold—" He broke off abruptly. "I'll be damned! Talk about luck!"

"What is it?" Toni asked, hearing the exultation in his tone.

"The man I was trying to keep an eye on," Adam

said in a low voice. "He's here. I could have saved myself some shoe leather."

"So what happens now?"

Adam frowned and then nudged her forward. "We sit down and have a drink—just as planned. Let's take that sofa with the good view. Comfortable?" he asked a minute later.

"You sound like a tour conductor." Toni moved to the end of the short sofa and shifted so that she could see more of the busy room. "Is it all right if I casually admire the scenery?" she asked, giving an excellent example of a young woman impressed by her lavish surroundings. It wasn't a hard role because the lobby bar area was as tastefully decorated as the rest of the hotel. There were thick carpets underfoot, and lustrous paneled walls behind the entertainer seated at the keyboard of a grand piano. Planters of greenery and palms were placed between the furniture groupings, aiding the illusion of privacy even though almost every chair was taken. Since the bar was really part of the lobby, it was possible to watch the bank of elevators as well as the transportation desk, and the lobby florist just beyond.

Toni was so intent on her survey that she wasn't aware Adam had given an order to an unobtrusive waiter until the man put down napkins on the low table in front of them and started for the bar.

"Coffee and Drambuie all right for you?" Adam asked, noting her surprise.

"Fine, thanks. Tell me, where's your friend now?"

Adam didn't pretend to misunderstand. "Over there talking to that gal at the transportation desk. He's the dark-haired one. Not too tall and on the slight side."

Toni managed a good look as she fussed over removing her blazer jacket and getting it settled around her shoulders. "He can spare a few muscles with that profile. He looks like a Spanish viceroy."

"Maybe there was one in his family tree. Although it's not anything that Benitez would advertise these days."

"Rafael Benitez?"

"Know him?"

"Hardly. Just what I read in the papers when he promotes island revolutions around the Caribbean. I didn't think he wasted any time in this part of the world." She took a sip from her liqueur glass after they were served. "Is that overweight man part of his entourage?"

"Damned if I know, but from his frown, I'd say so. Maybe he didn't want to leave Bourbon Street so early." Adam had shifted on the sofa beside her so that he could keep the men in his glance. It wasn't particularly hard since they were intent on their discussion with the ticket agent. When Benitez stretched out a demanding hand an instant later, the heavy-set man with a trimmed reddish beard reached in the pocket of his rumpled sport coat and pulled out a piece of paper. "Must be tickets," Adam said quietly.

"Maybe they're having trouble with their reservations. It would be interesting to know where they're going."

"My thoughts exactly." Adam watched a little longer and then relaxed as the two picked up their tickets again and headed for the elevators. Without wasting any time, he drained his glass and said, "Fortunately that shouldn't be too difficult to find out. Are you finished?"

His tone showed that if Toni was disposed to linger, she probably would be doing it alone. So much for her hopes that he'd been enjoying the last of the evening as much as she had.

The final proof came an instant later when Adam paid their bill and briskly helped her up. "If you don't mind, I won't escort you to the elevators," he said. "I'm going to have to work hard to get any information out of that gal at the transportation desk as it is. If she sees me go past with you on my arm now, there won't be a chance."

Toni's lips parted in amazement. "You mean you're going to ask her about Benitez and his friend? But why?"

"Because Rafael has recently been causing trouble on St. John in the Virgin Islands. The owners of a resort complex there are important clients of my firm. The way things are, they're having a hell of a time just managing to survive in the island politics—to say nothing of trying to enlarge their facilities." Adam's glance was focused a good two inches over her head as he added, "Thanks for the dinner, Toni. I'm sorry to rush you off like this. Give my best to Nora when you talk to her."

Toni managed to nod and keep a straight face as she murmured her thanks and walked toward the elevator. It wasn't until she was in the empty cage going up to her floor that she started to laugh helplessly. To think that earlier in the evening she would have repulsed Adam firmly if he'd tried another pass. She'd even decided to politely evade him if he attempted a good-night kiss in the empty hotel corridor. The only contingency she hadn't covered was a formal good-bye handshake in the lobby. And that was exactly what she'd received.

Chapter Two

It was barely nine o'clock when Toni entered the hotel's coffee shop the next morning and nodded when the hostess said, "One?"

She was led to a table by the wall in the paneled room and smiled in response as a passing waitress asked, "Coffee?" even before she could open a menu.

"Yes, thanks," Toni replied gratefully, and took a sip of the steaming liquid.

Just then, she needed all the help she could get. It had taken a long time to get to sleep the night before and when she'd finally managed it, her rest was shallow and disturbed. About six o'clock, she awakened with a start after a vivid nightmare. She'd been sitting in that red light hotel and Rafael Benitez's overweight friend had just bought her for the entire night. The two of them had climbed to a sleazy room where the pillows on the bed were erotic three-dimensional products from the Bourbon Street gift shop when she woke up shuddering. After that, it was hard to get to sleep again and she'd finally given it up entirely. Since it was too early for breakfast, she'd dressed and gone for a walk around some of the deserted blocks in the French Quarter.

There were a few delivery trucks in the narrow

streets and one or two shopkeepers out sweeping the grimy sidewalks, but the city was slow in awakening. At Jackson Square, where the tourists would throng later in the day, there was a handful of artists setting up their easels although most were talking in informal groups and sharing a breakfast thermos before getting down to work.

When Toni was on her way back to the hotel, she caught a glimpse of a tall, fair-haired man and her pulse speeded up until he turned and she saw that he really bore no resemblance to Adam at all. She told herself firmly to not be a bigger fool than necessary and after that concentrated on breakfast and how she'd pass the rest of the day.

She had ordered a waffle and was starting to read the headlines in the morning paper when a familiar male voice said, "You're hard to find."

Toni looked up to see Adam settling himself in a chair across the table. She waited until he'd been served coffee by a smiling waitress and then she said, "Won't you join me?"

Her quiet comment sent Adam's eyebrows up. "Sorry. I didn't know I needed a special invitation."

Annoyed at being put on the defensive again, Toni took a deep breath. "My fault. Blame it on the time of day."

"You don't look as if you got out on the wrong side of the bed." He surveyed her vibrant orange shirt-waist with one of those quick male glances that didn't miss a thing en route. "More like an ad for a high-powered breakfast cereal that's all vitamins." He broke off as the waitress hovered for his order. "I'll have whatever the lady's having," he said, nodding toward Toni. After the waitress left, he asked casually, "What *are* we having?"

"Juice, waffles with syrup, and sausage."

He looked more surprised than ever and she flushed guiltily, not wanting to confess that she'd indulged in calories because her morale was at a low ebb. Fortunately his only comment after that was to ask, "Would you like to read your paper in peace and talk afterwards?"

"All right—but I'll share. What will you have—headlines or the sports page?"

"The way I feel this morning, I'd prefer to skip the headlines," he said, reaching across the table for the sports section. "At least until I've gained some strength."

Before he disappeared behind the newspaper, Toni took an opportunity to complete her own once-over. Adam's features were finely drawn and there were lines at the edge of his eyes which weren't in evidence the day before. Even his well-tailored chino sports jacket which he wore with muted-brown plaid trousers couldn't disguise the fact that he looked every one of his thirty years just then. Toni saved her comments until the waitress put glasses of iced juice in front of them and had gone on her way. Then she said idly, "You look a little tired. Didn't you sleep well?"

"Fine—but not long enough. That ticket agent has worked swing shifts so long, she must be part owl. It was almost five before she decided to call it a night."

"I see."

Adam drained his juice glass and surveyed her dispassionately across the table. "Your talent for understatement is really something. Do you also see that

I've got a hangover that could qualify for the *Guinness Book of Records?*"

"Maybe you should have had aspirin instead of coffee."

"I've *had* aspirin, thanks. At this point, I'm hoping that food helps," he explained and disappeared behind the sports news again.

When their waffles arrived, he folded the newspaper and handed it back to Toni without any more discussion. She followed suit with the first section and was pleased to see that she managed to butter her waffle and pour syrup without dropping or spilling anything. At least Adam wouldn't know how disconcerting she found his presence across the table.

He seemed to brighten when he'd finished his breakfast and signaled for a third cup of coffee. "Now," he said, leaning forward in his chair and propping an elbow on the table. "I have a proposition."

Toni was stirring sugar in her coffee and her spoon clattered onto the saucer at his words. "Damn! I must have gotten some butter on my fingers," she said, trying to keep her voice steady. "Now I need a napkin and a new saucer."

"Did you hear what I said?" Adam's tone was ominous.

"Something about a proposition. What is it this time—another helping of go-go dancers? But it's a little early for them, isn't it? Especially the way you feel this morning. And besides, I'm your sister's roommate—"

"I had remembered," he cut in. "Although I don't know what the hell that has to do with it."

She shrugged. "Well, you said a proposition and that usually means just one thing."

"This isn't Bourbon Street and there are other kinds of propositions." He shot her an irritated look. "What kind of man do you think I am?"

Toni could have said that she hadn't the faintest idea. Especially since he'd shaken hands and practically bundled her into the elevator the night before in his eagerness to get rid of her. Her lips tightened as she thought about it. Somehow—some way—she'd make him pay for that.

She took another sip of coffee and let her glance come up to meet his. "You mentioned a proposition."

"That's right. You still have some vacation time left, haven't you?" At her nod, he appeared pleased, but he kept his voice businesslike. "Any special plans?"

"I've scheduled a visit to the bayou country and there are some plantations that sound terrific." She hoped that she sounded convincing. Actually, it was hard to wax enthusiastic about sitting on a tour bus by herself when the prospect was as enticing as an annual physical exam.

She must have been a better actress than she thought because Adam frowned and said, "At least hear me out. I need your help."

His words sent a flare of anticipation through her but she kept it hidden. There was only the slightest tremor in her tone as she replied, "Naturally I'll help if I can. What's it all about?"

"Benitez," Adam said flatly. "I discovered that he's on his way to the Caribbean this afternoon. First a stopover in San Juan, Puerto Rico, and then on to the Virgin Islands tomorrow."

Toni chewed on her bottom lip, trying to remember what she'd read about the Caribbean activist. "Isn't San Juan his home base?"

"Well, he was a local boy. Now he spends his talents stirring up the political scene wherever there's any kind of an election."

"Did the airline clerk tell you about his itinerary?"

He nodded. "Plus confirming that Rafael is traveling under a different name. It would be interesting to know if the American authorities are even aware that he's here—not that it's much of a trick to get a fake passport."

"You could report him."

"What's the use? He and his chum are leaving on the three o'clock plane anyhow," Adam replied with irrefutable logic. "No, all I'm concerned about is what Rafael's going to do from here on—especially on St. John in the Virgins. If there's any more delay in our clients' development scheme there, they'll be in bankruptcy court. Then one of Rafael's cronies can step in and take over."

"What can you do about it?"

"My bosses think I should be on the scene until the final negotiations are settled this week—just to look out for our interests."

"That makes sense, but where do I come in?"

"Everybody seems to feel that it would look better if I had a"—he hesitated as if searching for the right word—"a companion with me. You see, I met Benitez last year and he knows about my firm. On the other hand, there are lots of vacationers on St. John's at this season so you'd be the perfect cover."

"As your 'companion.'" Toni said the word just as carefully. "I see."

"You look as if you'd just found sour cream in your coffee," he said dryly and leaned back. "If it relieves your mind—this is strictly a business proposition."

"You mean with a salary?" Toni managed to keep the skepticism from her voice although she was curious to see how he'd wriggle out of that one. Business proposition indeed! At least she had to give him credit for a new approach.

Her mention of money made his eyebrows go up but just for an instant. "I don't see why not. Would you prefer an hourly rate or a package deal?"

His quick response caught her unprepared. "I—I—don't know. It depends. I've never done anything like this before. What would Nora think?"

"Who knows? Surely she's told you by now that I don't make a habit of ravishing her roommates."

"The subject was never discussed," she said, sitting up ramrod straight. "Besides that has nothing to do with it."

"Then what's bothering you? All your expenses will be taken care of—in addition to your hourly rate."

She frowned at his obvious amusement. "I don't know why you bother with me at all. Why didn't you ask your airlines clerk—the night owl who furnished all the information?"

"She has a fiancé coming in on a freighter this week," Adam said, dashing any hope Toni might have had that he simply preferred her company. His next remark confirmed it. "I suppose I could get a secretary from our main office if you don't want to go," he said and reached for their breakfast check as if tired of the discussion.

"I'll go."

Her words were out so fast that Toni was scarcely aware that she'd uttered them. Her eagerness must have been a dead giveaway to Adam but he merely nodded, seemingly engrossed in putting a tip on the table. By the time he looked up again, Toni hoped that the flush in her cheeks had subsided.

"Okay, I'll pick up the tickets a little later this morning and make our hotel reservations. We'll have to overnight in Puerto Rico and take a plane to St. Thomas tomorrow morning," he said. "After that, it's just a short trip to St. John. There's no use trying to stick too close to Rafael at this point. You're not the gumshoe type and he'd sure as hell be suspicious if I lurked behind a newspaper."

"Then all we have to do is take the same flights?"

"And look as if we're thoroughly enjoying our holiday."

"What about hotel rooms?"

Adam sighed. "There you go again. I'm beginning to think that you and Nora look under the beds every night." Before she could refute it, he said hastily, "Never mind. There will be perfectly acceptable accommodations. I told you earlier—this is a business trip. I learned long ago to keep my social life entirely separate."

His manner would have convinced her even if his brusque words hadn't. She decided to stop acting like a local Censorship Board before he changed his mind about taking her.

"What time do you want me to be ready?" she asked just as briskly.

"We should get the one-thirty bus to the airport. I'll make reservations for it."

His efficiency was so daunting that she remembered just in time to say, "The breakfast check. I meant to pay you for my part."

He appeared to consider it and then shook his head. "You're on the payroll—remember? Keep track of your lunch expenses and the company will reimburse you later. Any other questions? No? I'll meet you in the lobby at one-thirty then."

He was gone before Toni had time to gather up her purse, leaving her feeling as if she'd just survived a Louisiana tornado.

As she went up to her room, her feeling of bewilderment became tinged with a modicum of resentment. Even though she had agreed to his business proposition, she'd have to show Adam that he hadn't hired some meek little mouse.

One method would be to wear something more sophisticated, she decided, as she was packing her suitcases. Without hesitating, she changed her shirtwaist for a blue-and-green print trimmed in green suede. It fit like a dream and promised to be practical on the plane, besides. Her nylon raincoat could serve as a topcoat as well as protection if the gathering clouds meant business.

When she'd finished her packing, she found there was still time for a final walk around the Quarter. She set off cheerfully, knowing that it was a great deal more fun leaving New Orleans with things still to see. There'd be other times to visit the bayou country and look at plantation homes. She debated buying gifts in Jackson Square and then decided to wait and sample the duty-free shopping in St. Thomas instead.

Walking over to the Toulouse Street wharf, she leaned against a railing to listen to the steam calliope atop a big stern-wheeled river boat whose decks were crowded with sightseers. After that, Toni wandered through the French Market and weakened to the extent of buying a praline as she sauntered along. The city's weather was still muggy but the gray clouds looked as if they were content to threaten rather than cause a downpour. Toni kept her raincoat loosely around her shoulders and tried to decide where to lunch before she walked back to the hotel. She chose a side street in the French Quarter as she cut away from the waterfront, and started toward Royal Street, wondering what Adam was doing at that moment. Probably taking out his airline clerk before she went on duty, Toni thought, brooding over the prospect. She frowned as her imagination surged on, dwelling on all the possibilities beyond a simple lunch date. She was so intent that she almost jumped a foot when a male voice said, "No need to look so unhappy, lady. I can solve practically any problem."

Toni returned to reality in a hurry, staring at a long-haired man in stained, grimy clothes who lounged in a nearby shop doorway.

He gestured toward a display window that needed some soap and water, too. "Just pick out the one that fits your trouble."

Toni's glance followed, discovering that the entire display window of the tiny shop was filled with voodoo dolls. Her wide-eyed gaze moved to the shadowy interior of the shop behind the man where flickering candlelight illuminated an impressive row of glass jars along the wall. It was hard to make out their contents but she noticed some feathers and strange colored bones which didn't encourage further investigation. A strong smell of incense wafted out onto the sidewalk as she lingered, and unconsciously she identified a sandalwood odor, which was the pleasantest part of the entire establishment.

"Maybe you'd rather see the love potions. I have plenty of those inside." The shopkeeper managed a leer as he added, "Guaranteed to make a man do anything you want."

"Thanks, I'm not interested," Toni said, starting to move on.

"How about a doll to take home to your old man, then? It'll make him stay on the straight and narrow. One of those with the red cloth should do it."

Against her better judgment, Toni hesitated again. Her glance went back to the window where the unattractive dolls were propped against a piece of black material. The funereal color was entirely in keeping for they were a macabre display; their crude bodies were fashioned of dried flat reeds in the shape of a rough cross and the doll heads were constructed from a black felt hood with a garish red slash for a mouth. Some sort of plant material was used for black stringy hair and it spilled out of their crude cloth turbans. The main feature of the dolls, however, was the piece of material wrapped around them to form a rough bodice. Each cloth was stained with red where a heart would conceivably have been located and a long, lethal metal pin was stuck into the middle of the scarlet stain.

"I can give you a good price for two of 'em."

Toni heard the man's voice as if from a distance. Taking a deep breath, she moved her eyes from the almost hypnotic effect of the bizarre display. "No, thanks. Not this time," she said and walked purposefully on.

The shopkeeper's malignant look lingered with her and it was with relief when she turned the corner away from the store. She glanced overhead, as if willing the sun to come through the clouds to dispel the gray pall that held everything, including her emotions, in an oppressed state.

The sun didn't oblige and Toni frowned at the futility of it all. She sneaked another look over her shoulder to reassure herself that the shopkeeper was truly out of sight but her frown deepened as a bearded figure on the sidewalk half a block behind moved hastily into a doorway out of sight. Where had she seen the man? Of course—with Rafael Benitez at the hotel. Toni hesitated and then gave herself a mental shake before walking on. Damned if she'd linger to see if it *was* the same man! Probably it wasn't—and even if it turned out to be—what did it prove? Probably half the guests in the hotel were wandering around the French Quarter at that very moment with nothing on their minds except finding a restaurant for lunch. Her imagination was just running riot after hearing Adam's stories of Caribbean politics at breakfast time, and the sight of those miserable voodoo dolls hadn't helped!

She walked quickly back to the hotel after that and settled for a sandwich in the coffee shop before it was time to check out.

Adam was waiting in the lobby when she followed the bellman down with her bags at the appointed time.

"It's a blooming miracle," Adam announced a few

minutes later as he led her out to the curb to wait for the airline bus. "And living with Nora, too."

"What's so miraculous?"

"That you're on time," he said approvingly. "We're going to get along just fine. How was your morning?"

"Uneventful," she assured him. She was tempted to mention seeing Benitez' bearded friend on the sidewalk and then dismissed the idea. She still wasn't sure of her identification and Adam wasn't the type to appreciate flighty women with overactive imaginations.

At that moment, the airline van turned the corner and pulled up at the curb in front of them. Toni was being helped up the high step onto the bench seats even as she looked over her shoulder to make sure the driver was putting her bags into the rear luggage compartment. By the time Adam had slid onto the seat alongside, her thoughts of the bearded man had disappeared completely.

The entrance to the New Orleans airport was crowded with cars and taxis when they pulled up in front of it a half hour later. There was the usual delay of checking baggage and standing in the ticket line so that when they were finished there was only a short wait before flight time. Adam had purchased a paper at a newsstand in the terminal and offered part of it to Toni after they'd found seats in the boarding area. "Take your choice."

"You can have the front section this time. I'll have the comics and the classified."

"Not looking for another job, are you?" he asked as

he handed them over. "I should think two would be enough for any woman."

She opened the classified section. "I want to know what they're paying go-go dancers around here. There's a wide-open field."

"Planning on taking it up as a profession?"

"I don't think they'd have me," she said idly, folding a page back. "With all the drafts, I'd probably catch pneumonia during the first show."

"You could always put on a sweater for the second chorus. Well, what do you know—we've struck oil!"

His carefully casual tone brought Toni's paper down. "You're so right. Mr. Benitez plus his assistant—right on schedule. They cut it a little fine."

"Too damned fine," Adam said, consulting his watch. "I was beginning to think that Stephanie had the wrong computer readout."

"Stephanie being the ticket agent at the hotel?"

"Naturally," he replied impatiently. Then he grimaced. "Sorry. I forgot that you hadn't met her."

"I didn't expect to. After all, we're both just temporary help."

"What the devil's that supposed to mean?"

Toni was saved from explaining when the airline clerk at the check-in counter switched on the public-address system, announcing that their flight for Puerto Rico was ready for boarding. "Do we pretend that we don't know each other for Mr. Benitez' sake?" Toni asked, getting up and reaching for her carry-on tote.

Adam was still frowning over her other remark. "It's a little late for that. You're sitting next to me— remember? That was the whole point of the charade. We not only know each other," he went on, getting up beside her and putting an affectionate arm around her shoulders as they walked through the boarding tunnel, "we know each other very well. Remember that." The last was said in an undertone as they came up behind Rafael and his friend who were being greeted by a stewardess as she directed them to their seats.

"They're back in the next section," Toni reported a minute later after Adam led her down the aisle to their seats by the wing and waited for her to put down her belongings. "That means we can stop the charades for the time being."

Adam reached overhead to pull two pillows down from the overhead compartments and then settled beside her. "I'm aware of that, but I suggest that you do a little rehearsing before we arrive in San Juan. We're supposed to be flying off for a romantic holiday in the Caribbean. You looked as if you were headed for the guillotine when we came aboard."

Toni tried not to show how much his words hurt. Admittedly she had stiffened as Adam had moved near but it was in self-defense. If he'd been a little closer, he could have heard the way her heart was racing when he'd put an arm around her. Somehow she'd have to manage to be more convincing in her role-playing but it wouldn't be easy. Adam's profile was stern and unyielding as he fastened his seat belt beside her. After that, he accepted a magazine from a passing stewardess and started leafing through it, his attention resolutely on the printed page.

He didn't exhibit much more warmth during the three-hour flight. Toni could only think that since Benitez and his chum were out of sight for the moment Adam didn't choose to exert himself on his off-duty.

If she'd only realized, she was doing Adam an injustice. When Toni had stiffened under his hands in the airport terminal, he'd felt both guilty and annoyed. Guilty because he had apparently forced her into a position that she was regretting and annoyed because she didn't bother to hide her aversion. He decided not to interfere with her privacy during the flight except for bare courtesies. During the last hour when Toni apparently got tired of staring at the top of the clouds, she turned her face into a pillow and Adam grimly followed suit.

As the beginning to a Happy Caribbean Holiday, it left a lot to be desired.

Chapter Three

The pilot's announcement of their descent to San Juan brought them upright in their seats again an hour or so later. A few lights along the island coastline managed to penetrate the darkness which had fallen and the scattered pinpoints became a fairy-tale setting of colored glitter when the plane skimmed over the huge beachfront resort hotel strip on its final approach.

It was after nine o'clock when they deplaned at San Juan's big airport but there was still a great deal of activity in the terminal as passengers walked toward the baggage-claiming area. Adam managed a sideways glance down at Toni beside him. She had renewed her lipstick and run a comb through her hair but her cheeks were paler than usual and her eyes looked dark with weariness when she met his gaze fleetingly. In deference to his wishes, she was staying close but made no overtures beyond that.

As if aware of his thoughts, she said quietly, "Do you know where our friends are now?"

He shook his head. "Back in the pack somewhere. It doesn't matter. We can't do any more tonight. The important part will come when we get over to

St. John tomorrow. If Rafael sticks to schedule, we'll be on the same plane then, too."

"So all we have to do now is—"

"Find our hotel and maybe something to eat when we get settled in. How does that sound to you?"

"Good." His whimsical expression made Toni's tired spirits rise. As they went down a stairway to a lower level, she took a tighter grip on her small carry-on bag and said, "I wonder if Puerto Ricans have solved the baggage bottleneck?"

"I wouldn't bet on it." Adam's mouth took on sterner lines as he saw passengers from their plane mingling with a good many others as they waited for luggage to emerge on the conveyor belt which wound around the room. "Damn! It looks like a long wait."

"At least there are plenty of taxis," Toni said, standing on tiptoe to see beyond the claim area to a drive where lines of cars and airport vans were parked at the curb. "I think Rafael is getting into the first one. I wonder what happened to his fat friend?"

Adam had been behind a pillar when she first spoke and by the time he moved beside her, the taxi door had closed and the cab was pulling away. "You're sure Rafael was alone?"

"Practically positive." A frown creased her forehead. "Does that make any difference to us?"

"Hell, I don't know. We'll have to wait and see if they're together at the plane tomorrow. There are my bags. Keep an eye open for yours while I try an end run."

Toni kept her eyes glued to the serpentine of luggage which was jerking along on the conveyer by then but her two suitcases remained stubbornly elusive. They were still missing when Adam came back with his bags.

He raised his eyebrows. "No luck?"

She surveyed the items still unclaimed on the belt and shook her head. "Where could they have gone? It could be Rio or the Antarctic, I suppose."

"Nothing that drastic. We've only been gone a little over three hours. It's more likely they're still in New Orleans." He considered her purse and carry-on tote appraisingly. "Can you manage for a while with what you have?"

"I guess so. I'm fresh out of pajamas but I have my toothbrush and traveler's checks."

"Famous last words." He indicated his own bags which he'd left close by. "Keep an eye on those, will you? I'll go lodge a protest with the airline and tell them what hotel we'll be in. With any luck, they'll have found your luggage before long. Probably you'll have it delivered before breakfast."

He was back a few minutes later, shaking his head when she looked inquiringly at him. "They'll put a tracer on the bags but don't hold out much hope until morning. There's an early flight from New Orleans then. All the shops here in the terminal are closed— otherwise you could fill in a few gaps."

"I'll manage." Toni sounded resigned as he picked up his bags and they started toward the taxi rank.

"Sure you will. I'd offer you some pajamas if I had any along but I don't use them. At least it's warm enough so that the temperature won't bother you."

His announcement about his bedroom attire—or lack of it—startled her for a moment, but his calm follow-up about the weather gave her a chance to match his composure as they got in a taxi and started the drive to San Juan. "You're right about the weather," she said, leaning forward to open the car window beside her, letting the balmy night air blow on her face. "This feels more like July than March. Will it be this warm in the Virgins?"

"Probably. That's why half the people on the East Coast go there for midwinter vacations. Nobody minds the mobs if the alternative is shoveling snow."

"If that crowd at the airport here is anything to go by, San Juan gets its fair share of vacationers, too."

He nodded. "Gambling is the big lure in Puerto Rico. Plus the beaches, of course. It's too bad that you won't see more of the place."

Toni nodded as she glanced out of the taxi window. "So far it doesn't look much different from home. A freeway is a freeway and those neon signs in Spanish could be Los Angeles or Miami."

"That's why the old part of San Juan is so popular with tourists—at least for sightseeing." As Toni turned and looked inquiringly, he shook his head. "Sorry—there won't be time before our plane tomorrow. Maybe you'll have a chance to see it on the way back."

When their taxi pulled up before an impressive hotel in the Contada Beach section later, Toni stumbled from the cab, almost half asleep after the drive from the airport. She glanced hopefully at the small resort clothing shops by the hotel entrance but the only establishment open for business was a coffee shop, with a few patrons at the sidewalk tables.

"We can go over there after we register," Adam said, noting the direction of her glance. "Unless you'd rather try your luck at roulette."

"You mean there's gambling in the hotel?" Toni

asked, following him and a bellman into the big but almost deserted lobby. "It doesn't look as if they're doing very well tonight."

"The casino's up on the mezzanine. That's where all the action is. We can look in later."

It didn't take long to settle into their rooms on the upper floor of the hotel. Toni's bedroom was austere, with a double bed, bureau, and mirror plus one rattan chair. The adjoining bathroom was functional but its white tile and fixtures showed signs of age. Toni grimaced at her reflection in the mirror over the basin, thinking that her appearance fitted into the scheme perfectly just then.

Her mood cheered as she went back into the bedroom and slid aside the glass door to step out onto a small balcony. The view was so delightful it was almost unreal; moonlight illuminated a beautiful white sand beach below where waves approached delicately and retreated in the same way—like obsequious Victorian servants backing out of a room containing royalty. Further down, there was a sea wall to protect the palm trees along the shore. Toni was still standing there, entranced by their graceful silhouettes cast on the sand by the moonlight when a knock sounded on the door.

She walked across and opened it, keeping the chain guard on. Her cheeks reddened as she saw Adam in the corridor. "I didn't know it was you," she explained.

"Want to go down and sample the local color? After sitting so long in that plane, I need some exercise."

Toni smiled an acceptance and reached up to undo the chain barrier, motioning him over the threshold while she collected her purse and room key. "The view from the balcony's fantastic," she said. "Do you have one next door, too?"

He walked across to inspect the panorama and nodded. "Just the same. We're a matched pair." He bent down to test the mattress as he came back. "This must be stuffed with old sugar cane. I wonder if the people who buy these things ever sleep on them."

Toni was amused by his vehemence. "A firm mattress is supposed to be good for your back. I read it somewhere."

"Probably in the hotel's publicity brochure." He walked over to open the hall door. "I don't know why they bother—sleeping on the floor would accomplish the same thing." He cast a disparaging glance back at the bed. "There's not much in the way of blankets either. You'd better call the housekeeper after you get back."

"I'll be all right." She stared around the austere surroundings and tried to sound cheerful. "Once the air conditioning is turned off, it's bound to get a little warmer in here."

"You have more faith than I do. But then, Nora tells me that you're a paragon of efficiency." He closed the room door behind them, making sure it was locked before he gestured toward the elevators.

Probably he'd meant it as a compliment but Toni wished that he'd not dismissed her problems quite so casually. Which was absurd, she told herself, as the elevator took them back down to the lobby. She certainly could cope with that forceful air-conditioning system and lack of blankets. First thing in the morning, she'd also call the airport and see if they'd traced her luggage. It was all quite simple.

Adam's steps slowed as he led her through the deserted lobby where the desk clerk and bellman were engaged in a heated conversation over the switchboard. A hotel porter ignored them, too, as he leaned on a counter reading a newspaper, his broom propped nearby.

The man calmly turned to another section of the paper, prompting Adam to say, "At least he isn't letting his job interfere with his pleasures."

"Just think how lucky you were in hiring me," Toni informed him. "You don't have to worry about that while I'm here."

"You mean I'm getting a day's work for a day's pay? I had no idea you were so dedicated."

"Not dedicated—just illiterate. The newspapers here are in Spanish. That's why I'm not tempted."

Adam's eyes gleamed with laughter as they walked out of the building into the curving entrance drive. "I should have known. At least I'm safe for the moment. But it's not surprising that we could get rooms here at the last minute. This place has really gone downhill since they changed management recently. I guess it doesn't matter for one night."

"It's fine—and that beach looks heavenly." Toni tried to sound like the model of efficient and emancipated womanhood that he'd tagged her.

"Then I'll stop complaining. At least you'll be in for a treat tomorrow. The resort where we're going will make up for this and then some. It wasn't so easy to get a roof over our heads there." He took her elbow as they reached the quiet street. "That coffee shop looks like the only thing that's open in this neighborhood. Want to try it?"

Toni nodded and hurried to keep up with his long

strides as they crossed the pavement. The small coffee shop was the usual combination of vinyl booths and velvet wall-hangings but overhead fans were rotating slowly and they were met by a solicitous waiter who waved them to a seat nearby. The other customers were mostly drinking beer or coffee as they passed the time rather than bothering with food. When Toni saw how late it was, she wasn't surprised. And from the way two busboys were clearing tables and mopping the linoleum near the swinging door to the kitchen, it looked as if the restaurant was just about to close.

She gave the sticky celluloid menu a hasty glance when the waiter came over. "Just some soup will do. That shouldn't take long," she said.

"No hurry, *señora*." The man searched for a pencil stub and his order pad. "You like black bean? It's our specialty."

"Is there anything else?"

"Not tonight. The black bean is very nice," he said, writing it down as an accepted fact.

"Hold on . . ." Adam started to say, but Toni cut him off.

"No, it's all right. I like black bean soup. And I haven't had any in ages."

"If you're sure," Adam said, scrutinizing her across the table top which wasn't as clean as it might have been.

"And the *señor*?" The waiter continued as if there'd been no interruption. "Soup, *tambien*?"

Adam shook his head. "Beer. The local brand will do. That's all."

"And what will the *señora* drink?"

Toni kept her glance averted to avoid Adam's

mocking one. She knew nothing would be proved if she snapped, "*Señorita*," to correct the waiter. Obviously the man didn't give a damn! What's more, he probably thought he was flattering her. That was the trouble with Latin American countries.

Adam's voice cut into her thoughts, "He's asking you what . . ."

"I heard him the first time," Toni flared. Then she put her palms against her cheeks, aghast at her behavior. "Sorry, I was thinking of something else."

"Two bottles of beer," Adam told the man who nodded and disappeared through the swinging door to the kitchen.

After that, Adam kept their conversation on a carefully impersonal level while they waited for their order. He didn't appear concerned when silences occurred between them, seemingly content to watch the young Puerto Ricans sauntering past on the sidewalk. Most of them ogled the clothing displays in the tourist shops lining the streets but a few turned into a combination drugstore and news agent on the corner.

"If you need any last-minute essentials tonight, that's the place," Adam commented. "Unfortunately, the clothes section looks a little limited. From what I can see of the window display, you can either buy a T-shirt that says 'Souvenir of Puerto Rico' or 'Made in San Juan.' Not very original."

"I can imagine what the T-shirts will be like once we get to the Virgin Islands," she commented darkly. "It's just as well that I'm not the type."

Adam turned back to stare at her. The trim bodice of her dress was no protection from his raking appraisal which didn't miss one camouflaged curve underneath the fabric. "Why so modest?" he drawled when his gaze returned to eye level. "You'd have a hell of a time passing for a Girl Guide with your measurements. Five minutes in a T-shirt and you could enlarge your circle of acquaintances without the slightest trouble." His stern mouth quirked. "I'd give you odds on it."

Toni sat up straight, trying to retain a sliver of dignity when he was intent on destroying it. Too late, she became conscious that her action made her dress stretch even more tightly over the part of her anatomy in question and she blushed furiously.

"I've embarrassed you," Adam said without the slightest regret. "But at least I've proved that your normal reflexes haven't completely atrophied under that prim facade. And here comes your soup," he continued imperturbably before she could protest. "Just the thing to get your strength back."

Since the waiter was bending over the table depositing a huge bowl of chocolate-colored soup in front of her, Toni had to subside, seething. She waited until the man had placed the crackers within reach, poured the two bottles of beer, and gone on his way again before she said to Adam, "I'm perfectly all right. There's not a thing wrong with my physical condition."

"Exactly. That's what I was telling you."

"I don't mean that. I meant that I didn't need any restoring. Certainly not by you." She grasped her soup spoon and hefted it, as if uncertain whether to use it or throw it.

Adam leaned toward her, ignoring the danger. "That soup looks more like chili than anything else. I thought black beans were strained or put through a blender or something."

"So did I," Toni said, momentarily diverted. She tested the soup and confirmed that it was indeed a bowl of black beans with a little liquid around them. Her first swallow proved that the beans hadn't been left particularly long on the stove. "It's different," she said, taking a sip of beer.

Adam's attention was still on the soup. "The only time I've had it there was a thin slice of lemon on top."

"I know." Her voice was unconsciously wistful. "Or grated hard-boiled egg. It's delicious then." She took another determined spoonful so he wouldn't think she was complaining. "The flavoring is quite nice. I wonder what . . ."

Adam saw her spoon halt midway to her lips and go down again. "What's the matter?"

"Nothing. Probably it's just a piece of onion. You know how the outer leaves look like paper." She was discreetly trying to get rid of whatever-it-was on the edge of the saucer. Once she'd managed it, she started to take another bite when Adam caught her wrist. "What in the world are you doing?" she asked, as he took the spoon from her fingers and probed the middle of the soup with it.

"I was just wondering why they needed to leave the bean vine in for flavoring," he said, dredging it up for her inspection and then letting it sink again. "At least, I can hope it was the bean vine." He put the spoon down with dreadful finality and pushed the bowl to the far edge of the table. "I recommend the beer."

Toni nodded, leaning tiredly on her elbows as she picked up her glass. "Probably the soup was perfectly all right."

He shoved the crackers toward her. "Probably it was. On the other hand, we still have a way to go. We'll let some other tourist explore the chef's delight." His slow grin appeared. "Since you're short on wearing apparel, you're in no condition to receive a hotel doctor in the middle of the night."

They left the coffee shop a little later and strolled down the quiet street for a block or two, returning along the other side to look in the drugstore when they reached the corner.

Toni bought a postcard and a visitor's guide to San Juan before they walked back to the hotel. "So I can read about what I'm not going to see," she told Adam as they went in the lobby again.

"At least there's time for a flutter," he said, steering her gallantly toward the casino on the mezzanine where the hum of voices and the whir of slot machines could be heard. "After losing your luggage and surviving the battle of the black beans—you deserve a break. What will it be? Slot machines? Roulette? Name your poison." As she started to laugh, he added hastily, "Sorry. I didn't intend to remind you of that coffee shop again. In here, they get their pound of flesh another way."

He hesitated on the threshold of the casino and gestured to illustrate his words. The big room was crowded with people around the gaming tables plus all the customers waiting for a chance to try their luck at the lines of slot machines along the walls. The dealers at the blackjack tables and the roulette croupiers were sober-faced but their patrons appeared delighted with the action whether winning or losing. Certainly none of them seemed to care that the carpet was worn thin in spots or that there were dirty glasses stacked in the corners of the room.

"Maybe you'd rather skip the whole thing?"

Toni blinked and turned to find Adam looking at her quizzically. "I'm sorry. What did you say?"

"I wondered if you preferred to give it a miss," he replied, nudging her aside so that a new foursome could pass them in the doorway. "You don't look enchanted by the scene."

"My brain must still be on New Orleans time," she apologized. "Actually I was trying to locate the dime slot machines. They're my speed."

"In that case, we'll find the cashier and get some change. There's the cage back in the corner. And you can put your purse away," he added to her as they elbowed aside a portly gentleman parked by a roulette table. "It's all part of your expense account."

Toni opened her mouth to say it wasn't necessary, but before she could utter a word, a stunning redhead caught Adam by the arm.

"You wonderful man!" she enthused. "Why didn't you tell me you were coming back to town so soon? When did you get in?"

"Just a little while ago." Adam managed to evade her clutch and presented her to Toni. "Alicia Mills—Antonia Morgan."

The redhead managed a brief smile and nod before turning to Adam. "You must join us. Peter and Joyce are over at the blackjack table. They'll be thrilled to see you again."

"Hold on," Adam said good-naturedly. "I'll come over and say hello a little later. Toni's headed for a slot machine and needs some change."

"You don't have to bother," Toni told him, trying

to sound as if she couldn't wait to start on the one-armed bandit. "I have some coins in my purse. There's a machine by the door with no one waiting so I'd better stake my claim. It was nice meeting you, Miss Mills." She turned and walked back toward the entrance, trying to ignore the expression of triumph that had come over the redhead's face at her words.

Toni didn't risk a look back toward them until she'd pushed through the tables and established herself in front of the slot machine she'd mentioned. By then, the beauteous Alicia had maneuvered Adam to a blackjack table at the back of the room where he was being enthusiastically greeted by a well-dressed couple.

Toni turned determinedly to the slot machine in front of her. It didn't help to find it took quarters and she only had three of them in her purse. She fed them in slowly to make the process last longer but still managed to lose them in less than three minutes. Which meant that she'd have to go to the cashier's cage if she wanted to keep on playing. Unfortunately the grilled window was just a few feet away from where Adam and his friends ringed the blackjack table.

Toni's expression became more troubled. If she went to the cashier, Adam would feel obligated to include her in the group. She looked around then to see a young bar waiter lounging by the door. Toni beckoned to him and dug in her purse to find a dollar bill.

"Can I get you a drink, miss?"

"No, thanks. Just take this," she pressed the bill into his hand, "and deliver a message for me, please.

You see the tall, fair-haired man at that blackjack table over there?"

His glance swung to that end of the room. "I'm not sure which one you mean."

"The one talking to the pretty redhead."

"With his arm around her shoulders?"

"That's the one," Toni confirmed through clenched teeth. "Please tell him that Miss Morgan has gone to her room."

"That's you?" The boy was intent on getting the facts straight. "Will you be back?"

"No." Her retort was sharper than she'd intended. "I have a headache."

"Yes, miss." There was fleeting sympathy in his expression before he tucked the dollar in his pocket. "I'll give him the message."

And Adam could put whatever interpretation he wanted on it, Toni thought as she walked quickly out onto the mezzanine and was lucky enough to catch an elevator going up.

She didn't waste any time getting ready for bed once she reached her room. It didn't take long to hang up her dress and wash her nylon underthings. The air conditioner provided incentive, blowing frigid currents on her bare shoulders as she moved around in her thin slip which was to double as a nightgown. The deciding factor, though, was the chance that Adam might come pounding on the door, insisting that she return to the casino. Once she was in bed with the light out, she could truthfully say that it was too late. Especially since half her current wardrobe was dripping on the towel rack.

She slipped between the chilled sheets, carefully arranged her topcoat atop the thin blanket, and then let her head find the sturdy pillow. After that, she lay quietly, trying to keep her thoughts blank.

The first thirty seconds proved that was impossible, so then she concentrated on how fortunate she was to be spending the night in Puerto Rico instead of wandering around New Orleans by herself. It was only her perverse nature which reminded her that in New Orleans she would have had a nightgown, warm blankets, and an air conditioner that could be turned off at will. She was also by herself just then in Puerto Rico—a circumstance which Adam seemingly had no desire to correct.

Toni sneezed once and again. She debated getting up to find a handkerchief to wipe her suddenly wet cheeks but decided against braving the elements. Instead, she blotted her face on the edge of the sheet and then realized that she had to tuck the damp counterpane around her shoulders. It was either that or move to another part of the cold bed.

It was just too bad that she hadn't gone in that voodoo shop in New Orleans, she told herself in her misery. Probably they'd stocked a general-purpose voodoo doll somewhere in that ghastly display—one to cover tall men who fell prey to redheaded women. All Toni would have needed was a sharp pin to go with it—she could have furnished the instructions herself.

Chapter Four

The flight and unfamiliar surroundings must have taken their toll because Toni's eventual sleep was heavy and she felt almost drugged when a knock on the door finally roused her the next morning.

She pushed up on an elbow to see the face of her travel clock at the bedside and then frowned as the knocking was repeated more emphatically. "Just a minute," she called, shoving back the covers to get out of bed.

She was across the room with her hand on the doorknob before she remembered that her lace-trimmed slip was sheer, hardly the proper garb for receiving callers. "Who is it?" she asked.

"Bellman, *señora*. I have your luggage."

"Wonderful! Just leave it by the door, please," she instructed. "I'll get it in a minute."

"Okay." The voice had lost some of its eagerness. Possibly it had something to do with a disappearing tip. Toni decided that when there were two heavy thuds against the door and the sound of retreating footsteps. She waited a full minute then before she undid the chain lock, peering cautiously around the edge of the door. Her bags were sitting in the sunshine of the outside corridor where, beyond balustrades and archways on the far side, guests could look down on the hotel garden and big swimming pool.

Even as Toni dragged the larger bag into her room, she was thinking that it would be nice to start the day with a dip in that inviting blue water. Of course, she really should check with Adam to see if there was time for such frivolity. She debated that as she reached for her second suitcase. Intent on transferring it to a luggage carrier by the end of her bed, she nudged the door closed with her hip.

The prospect of being able to change clothes raised her spirits immeasurably and even the memory of Adam's takeover by the redhead the night before didn't seem as important in the bright new day.

She opened her balcony door far enough to take a deep breath of the warm air and decided a morning swim was too good to miss.

It only took a few minutes to brush her teeth and run a comb through her hair before she returned to the bedroom again, intent on unpacking her swimsuit from her smaller suitcase. She blithely opened the top of the case, and let it rest against the wall as she reached for the layer of tissue paper she'd packed around her best dress. Intent on finding the plastic bag with her swim things, she thrust the tissue aside. When her fingers suddenly came into painful contact with something sharp, Toni gasped and hastily pulled out her hand to suck her pricked finger. Thoroughly bewildered, she used her other hand to move the tissue-wrapped dress aside, giving a muffled shriek as she identified a garish voodoo doll in her belongings. She uttered another shriek as she heard the door open behind her and whirled to face the intruder.

"Don't wake the hotel," Adam warned and closed the door behind him. "What in the devil's going on?"

"Most people knock," Toni flared at him.

"I was about to when I heard you call out." He came over to her side. "You left the door ajar. What happened?"

Toni gestured toward her open bag and went over to sit on the edge of her mattress, her knees suddenly refusing to support her any longer.

"I still don't understand—" he began and then broke off as he saw the doll. "What's the matter? Did it come complete with a spider or something?" He picked it up idly to inspect it. "You'll have to wrap it better when you pack it the next time."

"I didn't pack it the first time."

"Otherwise you'll get some splinters from this cane—" His words trailed off as her comment registered. "*What* did you say?"

"That I never saw it before. I mean, I saw some like it but just from a distance."

"You're not making sense."

"The hell I'm not," Toni replied, losing patience completely. "Will you listen!" Adam's thick eyebrows shot up, but Toni didn't give him a chance to get a word in. "I saw a whole windowful of dolls like that in a voodoo shop in New Orleans yesterday morning but I didn't buy one. The strange part is that Rafael Benitez' partner—the bearded fat one— was around at the time."

"Why didn't you mention it?" Adam didn't sound sympathetic, simply impatient.

"Because I wasn't sure. I guess I just forgot about it."

At her obvious distress, his expression softened. "Sorry. I didn't mean to browbeat you." He hefted the doll in his palm. "You're sure you didn't pack it?"

"Does it look like the kind of thing anybody would forget?" Toni asked with unassailable logic. She stared grimly at the red-stained white rag tied around it. "The worst part is that just last night I was wishing . . ."

"What were you wishing?" Adam prompted when her voice faltered.

Toni knew she couldn't tell the shameful truth so she improvised. "Oh—well—I was wishing that I'd bought one as a souvenir."

"I can't see why—unless you wanted to stick pins in somebody." He took the long hatpin from the doll and examined it.

As he started to replace it, Toni drew in her breath sharply. "Be careful."

"My God, you don't believe in these things?"

"Not really. No, of course not." She shivered and folded her arms over her breast. "There's just no point in taking chances."

Adam gave her thinly clad figure a frowning scrutiny. "What are you sitting around in that slip for? You'll catch pneumonia at this rate." He stopped to toss the doll atop her bureau before plucking her topcoat from the foot of the bed and draping it around her shoulders. "Put your arms in the sleeves. At least it will do until you get dressed. I thought you were going to call the housekeeper for an extra blanket."

From his tone, he might as well have been chaperoning a troublesome ten year old. Toni caught a glimpse of herself in the mirror and felt an instant's annoyance. While she hadn't chosen to make a personal appearance in a satin and lace-trimmed slip, it wasn't the kind of outfit usually ignored by any red-blooded man. Adam needn't have shown such a pronounced lack of interest. Then, appalled to find the way her thoughts were going, she pulled her coat lapels around her pointedly. "There was no need to call anybody—I was perfectly all right." She sneezed in the middle of that self-righteous announcement, destroying its credibility.

"I'm glad to hear it." Adam stalked back to the doorway but lingered with his hand on the knob. "Your headache is improved, then?"

"Headache?" Toni clutched the coat even tighter, trying to think.

"The one that caused your hasty departure last night," he reminded her. "Or did I get your message wrong?"

"Oh, *that* headache." Toni chewed on the edge of her lip. "I felt better after I went to bed."

His sardonic glance swept over the hard mattress and the thin blanket. "Then you must have slept better than I did."

"Maybe just longer," Toni said, switching to the offensive. "Did you win any money with your friends?"

"A little. We can discuss that later. I'd like some breakfast—that's why I came by." His hand tightened on the knob. "Plus wanting to see if your bags had arrived."

Toni's eyes widened, her annoyance forgotten for the moment. "You knew they were here?"

He nodded. "I saw them by the reception desk when I was down in the lobby a few minutes ago.

Apparently they'd been dropped off at the hotel sometime in the middle of the night. I was trying to get through to the airline, so I had the porter bring them up."

"That was kind of you . . ."

"But I thought I'd better check and make sure they'd arrived. I got outside just in time to hear you."

She nodded hastily, preferring to forget that undignified shriek she'd let out when she'd discovered the doll. "I'll get dressed and be down right away."

"Right." He pulled the door open and hesitated a moment longer on the threshold. "They're still serving breakfast by the poolside. I'm sorry that we don't have more time so you could take a dip but it seemed more important to let you sleep."

Toni felt a flicker of resentment, noting that his hair was still damp above his brown sports shirt which he wore with a camel-colored sports coat and slacks. Apparently *he'd* found time for an early-morning swim. Maybe with the redhead. Was that why he'd been so solicitous about her rest?

"I don't want to interfere with any of your plans," she said stiffly after that disturbing possibility occurred to her. "Maybe you'd rather join your friends."

"We said good-bye last night. They were just acquaintances, anyway—so you needn't have worried," he said, as if he'd wasted enough time in explanations. "All you have to do right now is get dressed. I'll see you over a cup of coffee downstairs."

When he'd closed the door behind him, she heard him try the knob to make sure that it was securely locked before he walked away. Apparently Adam was still acting very much the protector.

A little later, she met him in the outdoor coffee shop and wondered if he was taking the role too seriously because he said, "I've already ordered for you. Scrambled eggs and bacon all right?"

Since the waiter was even then depositing a glass of orange juice in front of her, Toni nodded. "Whatever's easiest. It's beautiful here, isn't it?"

Sunlight was dappling the clear water on the far side of the big swimming pool just beyond the row of tables. A uniformed maintenance man was lackadaisically hosing down some plastic loungers and overhead the blue sky might have come straight from a Gauguin painting.

Adam gave the scene a cursory glance and then fixed his attention on her instead. "I like that dress."

Toni waited for him to say more but when it became evident that the calm statement was all that was forthcoming, she said in some confusion, "Thanks. I hope I judged the temperature right."

Since her linen dress also boasted a leather-trimmed sweater which she wore over her shoulders just then, her comment obviously didn't require any acknowledgment.

At least that was the way Adam must have considered it because he abruptly changed the subject. "I asked around in the lobby about your bags. The reception clerk just remembers seeing them at the end of the desk and all the bell captain knows is that he put them there. They were sitting just inside the front door when he reported to work."

"So we're back to square one."

"I don't think we ever left it." Adam watched the

waiter remove her empty juice glass and signaled another man who was passing with a coffee pot. When they'd both gone on their way, he shoved the sugar bowl across the table and indicated the packets of nondairy creamer alongside. "All the modern conveniences."

"Don't knock it. It's better than skim milk or old tired cream."

"I know. That's why I take mine black."

"Some people have will power. I believe in hanging onto a few vices with an iron grip."

When he grinned in response, Toni wanted to tell him that he should do it more often. It was wonderful to see his stern expression slip a notch. Just then his gray eyes were looking at her with approval which was certainly a first for the morning.

Unfortunately, his next words showed that he wasn't going to linger over trivia. "I take it that you didn't find anything new or unexpected in your other suitcase."

Toni shook her head.

"Could you tell if it had been searched?" he persisted.

"Not really. I never lock it because I lost the keys the first time I used the bag. If anyone went through my things, it didn't show." She shivered visibly. "I'm glad. One of those miserable dolls is enough."

"Even so, I think you should take it along. As evidence, if nothing else. Dammit—I wish they'd hurry with those eggs. That's why I ordered for you," he went on offhandedly. "I could tell that the speed around here is 'dead slow.' "

"I think the waiter's coming now." Toni offered mental apologies for ever thinking that Adam had been officious in ordering their meal. She could see from the impatient expressions of diners at other tables that he'd judged the dining-room staff accurately.

The eggs did appear and were almost hot which was more than could be said for the toast. Adam merely shrugged and said in a low voice when they were alone, "We can have something else to eat at the airport. There's no use flogging a dead horse."

She wasn't allowed to linger over her meal. No sooner had she put down her fork and taken a final swallow of coffee, than Adam was on his feet, tossing down his napkin as he rose. "I'll track down the waiter and pay the bill. You go on ahead and close your bags. This time you'd better wait with them until they're collected."

"If the airline would let me, I'd sit on them in the baggage section of the plane," Toni said grimly.

"They're probably safe enough now." Adam deposited a tip beside his plate and gestured her ahead of him. "Especially since nothing was taken."

"You're right. I must have hit the only thief in existence who followed the golden rule." At Adam's questioning glance, she explained, "It's better to give than to receive. Either that or he didn't care much for my wardrobe."

"It all evens out—you didn't like his choice in dolls. Where's our waiter?"

"He's over there having coffee with the cashier. You can't blame him—she's a good-looking blonde."

"Well, he can carry on his love life *after* he gives me the bill. I'll see you in the lobby later."

Shortly after Toni went up to her room and closed her bags, a bellman appeared. He picked up her suitcases and politely ushered her ahead of him to the elevator. When they reached the lobby, Adam had already corraled a waiting taxi. He watched the stowing of the luggage in the trunk with an eagle eye and then slid onto the worn seat beside her and closed the door.

Evidently he'd settled everything with the driver because they circled around a block and started retracing their route of the night before without a word spoken. When they'd driven for a time, Adam must have noticed Toni's wistful interest in the passing scene because he said comfortingly, "Maybe we can stop over here on the way back home. I'm sorry that you didn't have a chance to see the old part of the city and Morro Castle. It's a lot more interesting than this newer part of the island."

"It's nice just being here," Toni said as their driver slowed at a jammed intersection and then accelerated again. "Especially now that I have more than one dress."

Adam shook his head in mock reproach. "Women!"

"Exactly . . ." She half turned to face him. "As a matter of fact, I would have come with you without any mention of wages."

"That wasn't the way I heard it in New Orleans."

"Only because you weren't diplomatic in the way you asked me."

"Now she tells me," Adam said. "I'll make a note of it—flattery first, money as a last resort." He peered out the window as they approached the air terminal and then checked his watch. "We shouldn't have long to wait."

"The place looks mobbed this morning," Toni

said, seeing the lines of taxis disgorging passengers in front of the various curbside ticketing stands. "Do we leave our bags out here?"

Adam shook his head as the driver slowed to get in line. "There's no point in taking any more chances than we have to. Let's drag them inside to the ticket windows and see them on the conveyor."

There was the usual delay while they struggled through the tour groups and stood in line by the ticket window. It took still longer going through airport security when they found out that their departure gate was one in a far section of the terminal.

Toni was breathless from trying to keep up with Adam's strides as they walked down the long, hot hallway to it. "If we walk much further, we'll be off the end of the island."

Adam jerked his head toward a double door at the end of the corridor where the whine of jet engines could be heard. "This must be it. From the sound of things, I think we're right on the edge of the runway," he said. "Half a minute, I'll hold the door."

When they got inside, they found they were in what was obviously a temporary departure area. The small, roofed area resembled a carport more than an air terminal and air conditioning wasn't one of the amenities. Earlier passengers had filled all the rows of chrome chairs or were leaning against the walls. They stared with blank expressions at colorful mounted posters of the Caribbean showing passengers who were all young and smiling. By contrast, the ones in the waiting room were nearly all middle-aged and obviously sick and tired of sitting around in such a hole in the wall.

"There's been a small delay, but we should be

boarding shortly," a harried ticket clerk told Adam when he reconfirmed their seat reservations. She went down her list and spoke almost absently. "Only one still to come—a *Señor* Benitez."

If she'd announced a ticking bomb in the baggage stacked by the door, she couldn't have received a more surprised response.

"You *did* say *Señor* Benitez?" Adam asked finally, trying to sound casual.

"That's right." The clerk was reluctant to impart any more information and she shuffled her lists into a manila folder. "Wait by the door, please. We'll be loading right away," she added when a mechanic came and latched back the sliding door out onto the landing apron.

"I'll be damned," Adam said softly as he and Toni moved out of the way of the passengers who surged forward. "It never occurred to me that Benitez would stay on this flight. He was supposed to be angling for an earlier one."

"Why didn't we take the earlier one?"

"Because it was full—it wasn't important since we were all ending up at the same place this afternoon."

Toni was looking around the waiting room. "Well, unless he appears in the next few minutes or so, he'll miss this one. There's nobody new coming in except that little boy and his nurse." She nodded toward the back of the lounge where an elderly woman dressed in black was towing a dark-haired boy toward the desk.

The youngster looked to be about five years old but his slight frame made it difficult to be sure. There was no doubt as to his Spanish heritage; it was proclaimed with his olive skin and fine-boned profile. Combined with his outfit of a starched white shirt and short dark pants, he seemed almost out of a Goya painting.

"He doesn't look very thrilled about the flight," Toni remarked to Adam.

"Either that or he's not keen on that dragon with him," Adam concurred as they watched the stern-faced woman elbow people aside to reach the ticket desk. "Probably she's hoping for a standby seat. Maybe she can pick up the Benitez reservation." Adam shifted his carry-on bag and reached for their gate passes. "Things are thinning out, we might as well get on board."

Toni tried to follow him but found herself momentarily blocked by the nursemaid who was rattling Spanish to the ticket clerk. The clerk looked flustered by the last-minute commotion but shrugged as the woman gave her charge a perfunctory pat on the head and said, "*Adios*, Juanito."

"I'll be damned," Adam muttered.

Toni turned in surprise. "What's wrong?"

"Tell you in a minute," he said, taking her arm and marching her out to the steps by the plane.

Toni managed to disengage her elbow at that point. "What's going on?"

"That's what I'd like to know." He looked over his shoulder to make sure that no one could overhear. "It seems that Mr. Benitez didn't miss the plane after all."

"But I didn't see him—" Toni's voice cracked in the middle of her last word. She had to swallow before she could continue. "You mean that boy? Juanito something or other?"

"Juanito Benitez." Adam said, observing the ticket clerk as she turned the youngster over to a steward who'd been summoned to her side. "Must be a gathering of the clan."

Toni watched the sober-faced youngster approach. "Poor little fellow. He must feel as if he'd been abandoned. You'd think that his father could have gone with him."

"Exactly." Adam's expression was preoccupied as he followed her up the steps to the plane. "So now I'm wondering why in the hell he didn't."

Chapter Five

To Toni's surprise, when a steward met them at the door of the plane, he showed her and Adam to two seats in an otherwise empty first-class section.

Toni waited until he moved back to the coach area where passengers were busy strapping themselves in before she asked Adam, "Has he made a mistake or have we come up in the world? I'm not used to this luxury."

"Nothing's too good for the hired help," Adam told her, stowing his coat above the seat and waiting for her to sit down. "Actually, this is such a short flight that there's hardly time to have the free drink, let alone enjoy the extra room. Looks like we have company," he added in an undertone.

Toni glanced toward the door of the plane and saw the Benitez boy being hurriedly ushered down the aisle by another attendant. After a hasty glance around, the man gestured Juanito into the double seat opposite Toni and Adam. Without wasting any time, he pulled the seat belt around the boy and fastened it securely. "Take it easy, son," he told him. Straightening up again, he said to Adam and Toni, "This isn't my regular run and my Spanish is nonexistent. Can you give me a hand? The poor kid looks as if he expected the wings to collapse and I can't stay with him until after takeoff."

"Maybe I can help," Toni said, since she was in the aisle seat. She was on her feet before she thought to check with Adam but he nodded reassuringly when she looked down at him.

"Sure, go ahead," he confirmed. "Too bad we're not sitting three abreast so we could put him between us." To the steward he added, "Don't worry, we'll take care of Juanito."

The youngster stared wide-eyed across at them on hearing his name, looking even more bewildered when Toni came over to sit next to him. Fortunately the announcement about life belts by the steward in the coach section was made then, both in Spanish and in English so the youngster was diverted. By the time it was over, the plane was bumping along an approach strip to the main runway and the boy's fearful gaze went to the landing markers passing the window beside him.

Toni reached down and took his hand in a warm clasp, saying soothingly, "It's all right, Juanito. Pretty soon we'll be up above those clouds. See— there's just one plane ahead of us for takeoff." She deliberately kept her voice in a calm monotone and her bright smile didn't need translating. The boy's tense figure stayed stiff in the seat but she felt his fingers relax a bit as she went on, "There's the steward strapping himself in so it won't be long until we go 'whoosh.'" She gestured to emphasize the swift take-off and Juanito's firm little mouth quivered with laughter for the first time.

"Whoosh?" he parroted faithfully.

"Whoosh," Toni confirmed.

"Good girl," Adam said from across the aisle. "You've got it made."

And it seemed she had because Juanito's cheerful mien stayed with them when the plane rocketed along the runway and up into the vivid blue sky over San Juan. Down below, the Atlantic waters looked like an artist's palette in different shades of green and blue as the shoals around the myriad islands became apparent.

Toni leaned over Juanito's tiny figure so they could both watch the scene below. "Fishing boats," she pointed out. "Two of them."

"*Dos barcos*," Adam said, from across the way as he unfastened his seat belt.

"*Barcos*," Toni said to Juanito, passing the word on.

The youngster piped out, "*Barcos y pescadores*," and glued his nose even more firmly to the window.

Toni turned to give Adam's lounging figure a reproachful glance. "You should be sitting here."

He shook his head. "No way. You'll notice that he's still clutching your hand. You've picked up an admirer."

Toni's gaze went back to the boy beside her and her free hand automatically smoothed his glossy black hair. He looked up, startled, for a minute and then, reassured, turned back to the window. Toni sighed and glanced at Adam. "He's a darling. You'd think that his father could have taken him with him . . ." She broke off when the harried steward stopped by her to say, "There's just time for a drink before we arrive in St. Thomas. What would you like?"

"Oh, nothing, thanks." Then, seeing Juanito's bright, inquisitive glance, she changed her mind.

"Ginger ale, I think. Two ginger ales. My friend here will have one, too."

A few minutes later, Juanito was clasping a plastic glass, obviously enchanted by its icy, sparkling contents. Across the way, Adam lifted his scotch and soda in a silent toast. "It gets better and better. At this rate, you'll have trouble getting him off the plane."

"Do you suppose there's somebody to meet him in St. Thomas? And what about the launch crossing to St. John? He'll need help there."

"Stop fussing. I'm betting there'll be somebody on the spot as soon as the door opens. Remember that the nurse made sure he was taken care of before she left him at the airport."

"That old crone! She looked as if she had lemon juice instead of blood."

"Maybe. But you'll notice that Juanito was delivered in prime condition. Not a hair out of place."

"There are other things."

"For pete's sake, let's not get into child psychology. You'd better rescue that glass," he added firmly, "or those ice cubes will be in your lap."

"Oh!" Toni turned back to her charge to avert the catastrophe. "Finished? We'd better give these back—" She handed over their glasses to the steward just as the "Fasten seat belt" sign flashed overhead. "Look, Juanito—that's the island where we're landing. You can even see the strip—just beyond the houses out on the cliff. Do you see all those swimming pools? Umm—what a gorgeous spot!" The last was said to Adam as the whine of the jet engines changed and two thuds came when the landing gear locked into place.

"Just like Beverly Hills. Hang onto your friend—this is a short runway and sometimes they have to brake a little hard."

It was and they did but, thanks to Adam's warning, the jolt was over before Juanito had time to be frightened. An instant later, they were taxiing off the runway and the stewards were telling everyone to remain in their seats until the plane stopped moving.

"What do we do if there isn't somebody to meet him?" Toni asked Adam as the steward positioned himself by the door behind the pilot's compartment. "We can't just desert the poor tyke."

"Let's take it as it comes. First off, I'd suggest you unfasten his seat belt," Adam said. "The way he's wriggling doesn't need translating either. Juanito—*Ven aqui*." He put out his hand and firmly led the boy down the aisle to the restroom, cutting through the passengers with a purposeful stride.

By the time he was back, towing the smiling youngster, all of the passengers bound for St. Thomas had finished deplaning. "We'd better hurry or we'll go on to Miami by mistake," Toni said. "I don't think Juanito's family would approve."

The steward brought positive proof of that just a minute later when he came hurrying back from the forward door. "There's a lady outside pitching a fit about this young man," he said. "I'm supposed to deliver him to her on the double. Let's see, he didn't have a coat, did he?" Without waiting for an answer, he checked the empty overhead compartment and, finding it empty, gave a satisfied nod. "Right, then, we're on our way." He swung Juanito up in his arms again, "Say *adios* to your friends."

Juanito's lower lip started to tremble but before he

could break into tears, Toni reached up to pat his cheek softly. "Good-bye, Juanito. Take care."

"And so 'All's well that ends well,'" Adam said, as the attendant hurried out the door with his reluctant cargo. "We'd better go, too. Do you have everything?"

"You sound just like that steward with Juanito," Toni told him, hitching the strap of her purse onto her shoulder and clutching her tote bag.

Adam ushered her down the aisle ahead of him. "Probably because you look as if you'd like to break into tears, too. I don't blame you—he was an appealing youngster."

"You'd think that his parents could stick around to take care of him. Probably his father is too busy arranging revolutions and overthrowing governments. I hope we don't run into him; I'd probably say something I'd regret."

Adam paused at the top of the metal stairway and glanced down toward the straggling serpentine of passengers making their way toward the old-fashioned hangar which constituted St. Thomas' air terminal. "It isn't Rafael," he said.

Toni paused halfway down the steps. "What do you mean?"

"Just that there's some uniformed man carrying Juanito down the path and a woman alongside. Hired hands, I'd guess."

"Great," Toni said in disgust. "No wonder the little guy's a bundle of nerves. Oh, well, it's too nice a day to grouse. This place looks like a country cousin after Puerto Rico. I almost expect biplanes and pilots wearing goggles to come out of that metal hangar."

"Don't let appearances fool you. There's plenty of luxury in Charlotte Amalie."

"That's the main city here on the island?"

He nodded. "And it must be the cruise-ship capital of the world. It's not unusual to see eight to ten of them in the harbor at one time. The passengers come ashore for duty-free shopping."

"All the lure of Hong Kong without traveling so far." Toni followed Adam around the edge of the hangar out toward the taxi stand. Her voice was more wistful than she knew as she asked, "Do we stay here long?"

"Not this time." He was intent on flagging a small van and when it pulled up at the curb alongside them he asked the driver, "Can you take us to the Red Hook landing? We want to catch the afternoon launch to St. John."

The man looked at his watch and nodded cheerfully. "Yessir. We can make it if you and the lady just get on in."

"The lady will get in. I still have to pick up our baggage."

The black driver climbed down from behind the wheel. "Let me help you with it."

"I'll keep my fingers crossed," Toni told Adam.

"Relax, I saw your bags being put aboard the plane in Puerto Rico," he said, starting to follow the driver into the terminal.

"Well, if they haven't unloaded them here, that pilot is going to have an awful headache on the way to Miami."

Adam stopped and looked back over his shoulder. "How's that?"

She patted her tote bag. "That voodoo doll is wrapped up in here. I wasn't taking any chances."

A little later when Adam and the driver reappeared, Toni watched them store the bags in the back of the van and smiled at Adam when he finally slid onto the seat beside her. "No trouble this time?"

"Not a bit except for the heat in there. It must have been over ninety." He shed his coat as the van started off, draping it over the back of the seat before taking out a handkerchief to mop his forehead.

"It isn't much less out here," Toni said, rolling down a window, "but I refuse to complain. It's probably snowing back home."

"I know it is—" Adam shoved his handkerchief back in his pocket. "There's nothing wrong with this temperature; I just prefer it on the beach." He broke off as Toni gasped and clutched at him when the van driver turned onto the main road away from the airport. "What's the matter? You're white as a sheet." Then, as she sagged back onto the seat, he grinned and said ruefully, "Sorry, I should have told you that they drive on the left-hand side of the street here and over on St. John."

"For heaven's sake—why?"

"Maybe because the British were in occupation between the periods of Danish rule."

Color was coming back into Toni's cheeks. "What were the Danes doing here?"

"These were the Danish Virgin Islands until the First World War when the U.S. bought them," Adam explained patiently. "The capital was named Charlotte Amalie in honor of the Queen of Denmark—the wife of King Christian the Fifth."

"If I'd known I was coming, I would have done my homework."

He grimaced. "It would have taken you a while. These islands have had a rugged history. At one time, this place was the leading slave-trading center in the West Indies—at another it was home to pirates like George Bond and Captain Kidd. Now—the only attacks are on tourist pocketbooks along Main Street. Thank God, we won't be tangling with the hordes there for long. The ferry landing is just across the island, and after that it's only a half-hour crossing to St. John."

"Which is another island?"

"That's right. Another of the American Virgin chain."

"I don't see how it could be much nicer than this." She gestured toward the lush tropical foliage at either side of the crowded highway leading toward Charlotte Amalie. There were palms towering above them and colorful blooms on the bougainvillea and oleander planted for decorative hedges along the road.

Toni blotted the perspiration on her brow and took a deep breath. "You're sure we haven't missed a season somewhere? This place feels like midsummer. It *is* still March, isn't it?"

"Yes, ma'am." The driver beamed over his shoulder. "The climate's another big tourist attraction here in Charlotte Amalie. Maybe the city won't be so crowded when you come back from St. John. There are six liners in today." He gestured toward the town's inner harbor which they were passing just then. "All those cruise passengers do their best not to take any money home with them."

"And naturally the shopkeepers do all they can to

cooperate," Adam said dryly. He surveyed Toni's wistful face. "I'll bet you wouldn't put up much of a struggle."

She straightened on the seat of the van, trying to ignore the sidewalk vendors of coral jewelry as they passed the post-office square and turned toward the hills behind the town. "Do you suppose that Juanito is being taken to St. John, too?"

"Damned if I know." Adam was observing the crowded residential area of Charlotte Amalie where uniformed schoolchildren strolled in groups along the roadside. It took the strident horn of an open taxi-bus with its rolled side curtains to make the youngsters give way and let traffic resume.

Toni decided to abandon her efforts at conversation and went back to admiring the scenery. By then, the taxi had climbed up a twisting road edging the harbor, giving her a marvelous view of luxury hotels clinging to verdant hillsides and blue water inlets crowded with pleasure craft. Every type of boat from dinghies to mammoth cruise ships could be seen and, from the hilltop, they looked like child-sized toys on a blotting-paper sea.

The driver of the van hummed cheerfully as he tooled the vehicle along a busy two-lane road, waving occasionally to black friends when he passed them. He pressed down on the accelerator once they were clear of town traffic at the summit and started descending on the other side of St. Thomas' hilly spine. Instead of a busy urban area, they were suddenly driving past scattered land holdings with views over a trim landing area and dock. Beyond, out on the turbulent saltwater, a string of small islands looked like a pathway of rounded green stepping stones.

"That's St. John over there," Adam said, finally rousing to point out the biggest island some three miles away at the end of the chain. "It looks as if our resort launch is just coming in to the landing down below now."

"That's right, sir—no need to worry," the driver confirmed. "We'll be there in four or five minutes. You'll make it for sure."

"How many ferry trips are there to St. John?" Toni asked Adam.

"I haven't any idea," he replied. "I've always taken this special resort launch which pulls right in at the Calabash Bay dock. Otherwise, we'd have to get a cab from the ferry landing at the far end of the island."

The mention of private launches and docks made a shiver of anticipation run down Toni's spine. For the first time, she suspected that their destination was going to be considerably more elegant than the average resort. "This place—what did you call it?"

"Calabash. Calabash Bay."

She nodded. "This Calabash sounds quite something."

"Probably one of the top resorts on the international circuit," Adam said calmly. "Why?"

"I just wondered how you could get reservations on such short notice."

"This is something special." Adam was taking out a pair of sunglasses and he slipped them on as he explained. "When the directors heard that our friend was due, they were glad to have reinforcements for their side. As far as reservations go, I know for a fact that we'll have to take whatever's available." He reached for his wallet as the van arrived at the bottom of the hill and they turned into a neatly landscaped boat landing. "Let's hope that 'whatever's available' doesn't turn out to be two broom closets over the kitchen ventilator."

The driver was braking then in front of the Red Hook landing which was staffed by members of the U.S. Park Service. Toni wasn't allowed to linger long enough to read about the Virgin Islands on the notice boards at the modern information center. Adam barked out a "Come along" as soon as he paid the cab driver and led her down a wooden dock while a porter brought up the rear with their baggage on a cart.

Toni dog-trotted behind in a way that self-respecting squaws had abandoned years before. She felt like telling Adam that it was a good thing Rafael Benitez wasn't around because he'd never believe that she was more than a casual acquaintance or minor employee. Especially a minute later when she was forcefully propelled over the railing of the Calabash launch onto the heaving deck. When she opened her lips to protest, she got a mouthful of salt spray as a wave hit the side of the boat.

Adam kept his firm grasp on her arm, as he shoved her into the cabin an instant later. "You'll get soaked if you stand around on the stern," he said. "Didn't anybody ever tell you to come in out of the wet?"

"Not recently." She managed to keep her voice on a conversational level but her glance was mutinous as she massaged her arm. "If this keeps up, I'm going to put in a claim for health insurance. I didn't have to be handled like a sack of potatoes. I could have made it aboard on my own."

"Not at the rate you were going. This is their last trip for the day." Adam jerked a thumb toward the burly crewman who was already coiling lines while the helmsman opened the throttle. The launch's powerful engines roared as they left the dock.

"They wouldn't have left me standing there," Toni said. She was still indignant but it was hard to maintain her annoyance as the launch plowed out into the chop of the channel.

"Here—sit down before you . . ." Adam's voice trailed off as he suddenly realized that his comment wouldn't improve her mood. "It can get rough when we reach open water," he finished diplomatically. He kept behind her, shoring her up until she could reach a padded bench at the side of the launch. "Damn! I forgot to ask if the motion bothers you," Adam went on, appraising her pale cheeks. "I could have given you a pill."

"You don't have to treat me like Juanito." His obvious concern made her take stock, for as the launch surged even faster, the bottom of the hull was smacking the tops of the waves like an iron hammer. Toni realized to her horror that her stomach wasn't taking kindly to the battering-ram effect. A few minutes later, when the helmsman changed course, they were caught in the wake of a local work boat and the Calabash craft wallowed in deep troughs.

The combination was disastrous for Toni. She turned a mute, imploring face toward Adam.

"This way," he said, springing up and towing her by the arm again out to the stern rail.

When they reached it, her queasiness had blessedly subsided, but she stood there a minute or two just in case, keeping her eyes closed against the ominously surging waves. Then she felt Adam pushing her back inside and a moment later a cold, wet handkerchief was mopping her face.

"Plenty of saltwater out there," Adam explained when she opened her eyes again, "so I borrowed a little. You'll be okay now—it's just been too much, too fast. Sit back and relax."

Toni was beyond feeling embarrassed. She took the handkerchief from him and wiped her hands. There were two choices at that point, she reflected wryly. She could throw herself over the rail and thereby never have to face the man again or she could behave like a rational human being and forget the whole thing.

"Thanks for your help," she told him gravely. "Believe it or not, I've never even felt seasick before. You certainly have fast reflexes."

"Well, you were an interesting shade of green. I recognized the color because I've been in the same predicament. Just ask my sister about our first family fishing trip or—better still—don't."

"I wouldn't dream of it." She looked around and was comforted to see that both of the crew were on the bridge, their attention straight ahead. Toni let her gaze come back to Adam at her side. "I'm glad that there weren't any other passengers to witness my mad dash."

"I'm surprised there weren't. Oh, not the dash"—he grinned companionably—"but that we're the only ones aboard. Usually guests from Calabash come into St. Thomas for the shopping. Of course, with weather like this"—he gestured toward the sunlit water—"most of them stay on the beach."

Toni was rummaging in her purse for her waterproof cosmetic bag and tucked Adam's wet handkerchief inside. "I'll return it later," she murmured before asking, "Will we have time for the beach?"

"You will. There are a few people I have to see." Adam patted her arm and then withdrew his hand.

In companionable silence, they watched the almost steady stream of sailboats and cruisers which passed for the rest of the crossing. As their launch neared St. John, Toni could see the long white sand beaches for which it was noted. They headed in toward one in the middle of the island—a level area with towering palms. At either end of St. John, however, the land rose to higher elevations with hillsides thickly covered in deep-green vegetation. The contrast in colors between the green plant life and the unsullied blue of the sky, rimmed with the variegated greenish-blue shades of the shoal waters, made a breathtaking scene.

As the launch cut speed to ease alongside the wooden jetty, Toni turned to Adam and said wistfully, "It's perfectly gorgeous. You've ruined me forever. From now on, every time the temperature falls at home, I'm going to think of this heavenly place. All it needs is a sign marked 'Paradise' at the end of the jetty. And maybe some gorgeous women in grass skirts coming out to meet the boats."

"You're in the wrong ocean. I think you've got it mixed up with Tahiti or Samoa."

"Who cares—it's all the same."

He rubbed his chin. "Not quite, unfortunately. The Caribbean's simmering with political fires right now. Behind that peaceful shoreline, there's more going on than you could believe. That's why Benitez is finding such an audience for his spiel. All he has to do is mention what's happened in the past—like that bloody uprising of slaves here in the summer of 1733.

It took almost an entire year for the Danes to stamp out the revolt. Even then, the plantation owners needed two French warships and a company of soldiers from Martinique." Adam stood up as the launch bumped gently against the side of the jetty and the crewman jumped ashore with the bow line. "I'll tell you the rest another time. Are you feeling back to normal, now?"

Toni got up and reached for her raincoat and purse. "Yes, thanks. You took my mind off everything with your 'bloody uprisings.' Surely you're not suggesting that . . ."

"The same thing's going to happen now? Hell, no! Any struggles these days are more apt to be for economic control."

"That's reassuring." Toni watched their luggage being swung over the rail onto the jetty and then saw a uniformed porter ambling down toward the launch with a baggage trolley. "All the comforts of home."

"I should hope so." Adam nodded his thanks to the crewman as he was assisted ashore and turned back to help Toni up onto the wooden dock.

For an instant she had trouble making the planks stay steady under her feet and then she took a deep breath of relief when they settled into place.

"All right?" Adam was gazing at her in some concern.

"Yes, thanks." She fell into step beside him as they walked along the jetty toward the administrative center of the resort. On either side, there were white sandy beaches tenanted with scattered bathers, some of whom were watching a man trying to right a sailboard which he'd capsized by the jetty. Most of the guests were stretched on their loungers, solely intent on improving their suntans. Practically nobody was watching the arrival of Calabash's two newest guests.

Toni and Adam reached the end of the jetty and followed the man with their luggage toward some low buildings almost hidden in the palm thicket. As they neared them, a few more guests converged on the winding walk. The porter moved in their wake, going toward the only structure which boasted two stories.

"Are you sure that this place is fully booked?" Toni asked Adam in an undertone. "It looks to me as if you'd have trouble fielding two teams of softball."

"That's the object of the management. No crowds on the beach, no radios or television, and three incomparable meals a day."

"At a price?"

Adam chuckled. "I should say so. But there are lots of people more than willing to pay for such luxury."

"This doesn't look very posh," Toni said, nodding toward the rough-cedar exterior of the building in front of them which bore a discreet 'office' sign beside its open door. But when they got inside and she saw the luxurious leather furnishings in the small reception area, she muttered, "Oh, oh—I think I spoke too soon."

Adam grinned and waved her over to sit in one of the chairs while he registered with the dignified olive-skinned man behind the counter.

"Mr. Driscoll and Miss Morgan," the reception clerk read as Adam gave him the completed card. "We were expecting you. Fortunately, we were able to move one of our other parties around so there'd be available space."

"I hope it didn't inconvenience anyone," Adam said.

"The instructions came from our main office, Mr. Driscoll," the man told him. "They were very specific." He imparted the information without emotion. To Toni, who was listening, it sounded as if the desk clerk would have preferred telling them to go to blazes but he knew better than to try. "You'll have cottage one twelve," he went on, putting a diagram of the resort down on the counter. "Would you like one of the boys to show you the way?"

"Thanks, we'll manage by ourselves," Adam said, pocketing the two keys which were offered with the diagram. "I'd like to see Mr. Nicholas first if he's free."

The clerk's eyebrows went up. "I'm sorry, Mr. Driscoll. Our manager's been on sick leave recently and he's not expected back for a month. We have a new man from Puerto Rico taking his place—a Mr. Benitez. Is there anything he can do?"

Chapter Six

Toni was stricken on hearing the desk clerk's announcement but she wasn't any more flabbergasted than Adam who gave the appearance of a man stunned with a blow to the solar plexus.

"Did you say Benitez?" he finally managed to ask the clerk.

"Yes, sir. But he's not in just now—he had some personal business at Cruz Bay. I can make sure that he gets in touch with you when he returns."

Adam, on the point of agreeing, fell silent when Toni tugged at his coat sleeve. Looking down, he saw her give a slight, almost imperceptible shake of her head. When he raised his glance to intercept the desk clerk's puzzled one, he said, "Don't bother. It isn't important. I'll get in touch with him tomorrow or the next day." He took Toni's hand. "C'mon, darling, let's see what our rooms are like. There's still time for a swim."

Adam hardly waited until they were clear of the building and on the curving walk which led along the beachfront before he drew up. "Now, then—what the devil was all that about?"

She looked over her shoulder to make sure that they

weren't being followed. "You have the wrong Benitez, that's all."

"What are you talking about?"

"There was a name on the desk at the back of the room. Jorge Benitez—not Rafael."

"I saw it when we were leaving but I still have to learn what the connection is." Toni's crestfallen expression made his tone soften. "It's probably a good thing you spoke up when you did—there might be a better way than the direct approach. I'll call the home office to see if the directors know what's going on here. We might as well check into the room first, though, before I go down and phone."

"Go down?"

"That's right. Remember—there aren't any phones in the rooms. I hope that doesn't bother you for a few days."

Toni pulled back when he would have walked on. "You have to be kidding! It's just a pity that Calabash is involved in a political seesaw." She waved a hand at the exquisitely tended grounds on either side of the walk. "This place is so perfect that it's almost unbelievable."

"That's what makes it worth the struggle." Adam started on down the path, tossing his raincoat carelessly over his shoulder. "The developers spent a fortune to achieve this 'natural' effect. Each group of cottages is almost hidden yet they all have an uninterrupted view of the beach. Our suite should be right along here," he added, checking the number of the key in his hand.

Toni trudged dutifully beside him, her attention on some flat-roofed bungalows faced with native stone just ahead. She hadn't had the nerve to mention their sleeping arrangements in front of the desk clerk and Adam's assured manner made her hesitate to ask even then.

If there was just one bedroom, probably there'd be a couch somewhere else, she told herself, although she couldn't let Adam know that she was concerned with such trivia. She'd already made a fool of herself by her antics on the launch. Any more idiotic behavior and he'd send her back to St. Thomas.

Evidently Adam attributed her silence to awe at their surroundings because he was content to let it lengthen as they approached the end cottage. He bent to insert the key in the lock and gave a mutter of satisfaction when the door opened smoothly.

Toni echoed his approval when he gestured her ahead of him into the main room. The design scheme of the suite was in muted grays and browns plus touches of oyster at the draw curtains edging floor-to-ceiling windows on the beach side. The wall beside them was entirely native stone, providing a unique texture behind the simple wooden headboards of twin beds pushed together to form a king-sized surface. Overhead, big brass ceiling fans turned lazily to provide a welcome current of air. Toni started to frown but her worried look eased when she walked past the occasional chairs in the middle of the room to discover a double bed at the far end. With some relief, she noted a plastic room divider which could be pulled to screen off that sleeping area.

If Adam noted her lightened expression, he didn't let on. "The bath's in here," he said, gesturing toward another door. "Only one but that shouldn't be any problem. This glass door opens out to a private porch," he continued, walking across to pull aside one end of the curtain.

Toni went over beside him, drawing in her breath with delight as she gazed out onto one of the prettiest beaches she'd ever seen. The sand was fine and white, leading down to azure water which surged up in gentle waves. Towering palm trees framed the idyllic scene, together with an almost cloudless blue sky.

"It's out of this world," she said reverently. "And that looks like a shallow dropoff, too."

Adam nodded. "No problems and no undertow. Plus a cove full of every kind of tropical fish. Just take a slice of bread with you and they'll eat out of your hand."

"You mean it?"

"Absolutely. The marine life is fabulous around here. That's why the famous underwater nature trail is just up the coastline a ways at Trunk Bay. I wish I could stay around and show you but I'd better get on with my phoning."

"At least you had a swim this morning in San Juan."

He looked puzzled. "Where did you get that idea? There wasn't time for more than a shower."

So she'd maligned him unfairly at breakfast, too, Toni thought ruefully and wondered if she'd ever learn. "Well, this beach looks simply heavenly," she said, trying to make amends. "I may never get out of a swimsuit all the time we're here."

"There are a couple of drawbacks to that idea, but don't worry about them now."

"My feeling exactly," Toni told him with a smile, "unless they involve killer whales or hammerhead sharks—I refuse to listen." She let the curtain fall back and walked over to put her purse on a bureau. "Where do I stay?"

"You mean for sleeping?" Adam asked, frowning. "You pick a bed—it makes no difference to me."

"I know that—but I'm still supposed to ask."

"Well, now you've asked," he said laconically. "I can't see what the fuss is about. Once you pull that room divider"—he gestured toward the vinyl curtain—"you're on your own. Sleep on the floor if you'd prefer."

"I'll take the double bed," Toni announced, deciding that he'd had enough raillery at her expense. She moved her purse from the bureau to a table by the bed and frowned at an object beside it. "An ice bucket?"

"Just one of the conveniences." Adam gestured toward the small desk where another ice bucket reposed. "Somebody comes in to fill them twice a day. They bring afternoon tea, too, if you want it."

"I'd settle for a sandwich. Is there anything as plebeian as a late lunch?"

"After that boat ride, I wasn't sure whether I should mention food." He hesitated and then asked, "Would you mind eating alone? There are three restaurants you can choose from."

"One will do." Toni tried to sound brisk and uncaring. "You go ahead—I'll wait for the bags to arrive and unpack first. Can I do anything for you—in that line?"

"You don't have to spell it out." Adam was irritable suddenly. "I'm well aware of your terms of employment but I'd be grateful if you'd forget them for a while. Just take it for granted that I'm not planning to pounce on you or slash the screen. You're here for effect and that's as far as it goes." As he headed for the door, he added, "You'll probably feel better after you have something to eat. I'll try to join you if I can get through with my calls but don't count on it. At least, we might manage a swim later on."

"To keep up the illusion?"

Toni's question caught him halfway over the threshold. He lingered long enough to say, "That's right—now you're getting the idea," before he slammed the door behind him.

She stood immobile for a moment and then stuck her tongue out at the solid wood barricade. It was a childish gesture but if Adam persisted in treating her like an *enfant terrible*, she might as well throw herself into the role.

She pulled her tongue back hastily, however, when a knock sounded on the same door. Moving over to answer it, she found a porter with their luggage and waved him in. He stored all their things on the floor beside the twin beds but Toni moved her suitcases as soon as he'd left the suite. Her bag was put on a luggage rack at the far end of the room and she carefully stowed her smaller bag in the closet next to the double bed. After that, she unpacked her cosmetics from her tote bag and, in the process, ran across the voodoo doll which she'd carefully swathed in tissue before leaving Puerto Rico. She surveyed the sharp pin which was stuck in the wrappings and almost yielded to another childish impulse. Sanity prevailed and she put the doll back in a suitcase, away from temptation.

As she renewed her makeup in the gleaming tiled

bathroom, she felt a rising sense of excitement as well as a decided appetite for lunch. After all, she was in a gorgeous resort, enjoying a free vacation, and Adam wasn't going to spoil a bit of it with his overbearing manner.

She thought about changing her clothes and then decided to wait until after lunch. Probably by that time she'd succumb to lazing on the beach rather than exploring the resort, but there was certainly no hurry to make up her mind. She did slip on a pair of cork-soled espadrilles before letting herself out the front door.

There was a chambermaid on the walk nearby who was glad to tell Toni all she needed to know about luncheon spots. "The closest place is the Tower," the uniformed girl informed her, gesturing toward a big thatch-roofed structure on a slight rise behind the reception buildings. "Of course, there's the main dining room on the beach next to the pier, or the harbor dining area up the road. You'd need to take the shuttle bus for the last one, though."

"Where do I catch the shuttle bus?" Toni wanted to know.

"Down by the foot of the Tower. It leaves every half hour and circles the resort."

"Well, if I'm going over to the Tower, I might as well have lunch there," Toni decided aloud.

"I would, ma'am. Especially since you just missed the bus." The maid indicated an open-air van disappearing over a rolling hill behind them. "It's on the way to the Harbor section right now."

"Then I'm on my way to the Tower," Toni said, smiling her thanks.

She set out on another hard-surfaced path which

angled toward it. Apparently the structure had been patterned after an old sugar mill with a conical thatched roof. Its stone walls were covered by flamboyant bougainvillea and the pink and orange blooms stood out in glorious profusion against the gray background. Diners were seated so they could enjoy the flower display as well as a commanding view of the shoreline.

It was such an arresting sight that Toni almost missed seeing the small boy who was trudging down a path toward the reception area, carefully supervised by a uniformed girl. It was the youngster's formal attire which made Toni do a double-take and she hesitated, undecided whether she should call out. By then, the boy's attention was on a little brown animal with a bushy tail which was bounding across the lawn between them. An instant later, it was Juanito who recognized her when the animal scurried behind a nearby palm tree and his gaze traveled to her motionless figure. A shy smile brightened his face and he piped out, *"Señora!"* in a determined voice.

"Hello, Juanito!" Toni called across the lawn. She would have gone over to talk to him except that the nursemaid gave her a quelling glance at that moment and marched the boy on down the path toward the beach. "Well, for heaven's sake," Toni muttered to herself as she stared after them. "So much for the friendly Caribbean." Then she rationalized that the nursemaid was simply doing her job. Making sure that her charge didn't talk to strangers probably headed her instructions.

Toni walked on along the path toward the restaurant, deciding that the next time she saw them, she'd explain to the nurse that she merely wanted to renew an acquaintance. Certainly the poor youngster looked as if he needed a friendly face somewhere in his life!

A uniformed maitre d' met her at the top of the Tower and conducted her to a shaded table by the wall without delay. Toni raised her eyebrows at this formality in such a casual setting, for a quick look at the menu showed that salads and sandwiches were the specialty. When a tall waiter came to take her order, Toni chose a fruit salad and asked for iced tea right away. It was scarcely delivered before a man's voice behind her said in pleasant, but firm, accented tones. "And how is it that you know my son, *señorita?*" As Toni turned to look, he moved around and stood by the table. "It seems strange because I'm sure we haven't met. My name is Benitez—Jorge Benitez." His voice dropped expectantly, waiting for her reply.

The man's sudden appearance was only partially responsible for her breathlessness as she said, "I'm Antonia Morgan. We've—I mean—I've just arrived. You're the manager here, aren't you?"

He gave her a smile of pleased surprise. "Again you have the advantage of me. May I join you for a few minutes, Miss Morgan? I feel sure we must have more in common than a shared interest in Juanito."

He took her consent for granted, already arranging for another chair. It gave her a chance to observe him as he directed the hovering waiter. She immediately decided that women must have been staring at the man for the better part of his thirty or so years. Not that his overall physical appearance was unusual; he was of medium height and slight, wiry build, but from there the word "average" changed to "superlative." His profile could have been used on a Greek coin—with fine features and slumberous dark eyes which combined to make him look like a matinee idol. Sleek dark hair worn only slightly long over an immaculate white shirt collar completed the illusion.

There was enough of a resemblance to Rafael Benitez that the men had to be related, Toni decided. Maybe if she was able to steer the conversation into the proper channels she could steal a march on Adam, after all.

It was difficult to keep excitement from her voice as she smiled across the table at him. "I didn't mean to cause any worry when I spoke to Juanito, Mr. Benitez. We traveled on the same flight from Puerto Rico today. I was happy to see him again—he's a darling boy!"

The manager's thick eyebrows went up in surprise. "Of course—and you're the beautiful lady he talked about all the way from Cruz Bay."

"Cruz Bay?"

"Where the seaplanes land. I had Juanito flown over from St. Thomas a little while ago. It seemed easier than bringing him by launch."

Easier for whom, Toni felt like demanding, as she felt a surge of pity for Juanito. The child had been petrified during the initial stages of their first flight; it wasn't likely that he would have changed in a smaller plane.

Her supposition was apparently accurate. "He hasn't been happy since his arrival," Juanito's father admitted. "All he'd swallow for lunch was a glass of milk. I have a feeling that he would have resisted taking his nap if I hadn't promised that he could have a swim later."

"Probably he's just tired," Toni said, knowing

better than to offer any advice on child-raising. "And having everybody speak English on the plane might have confused him."

"I don't see why. His Puerto Rican nurses have been instructed to use both languages since he was a baby." Benitez spoke with an assurance which didn't bear contradicting. "Even my wife knows that she is to use English some of the time."

"Then Juanito will soon pick it up. Especially when you speak it so well, too."

"It's not surprising. I went to a university in Florida."

She smiled to cover her embarrassment. "I should have known. Was that the custom in your family?"

"Only for my brother and myself. Rafael was just there for a year, afterwards he went on to Europe. That often is the rule for families in this part of the world."

"It sounds very pleasant." Probably it was too much to hope that he'd disclose much more of the family history but she could continue with her discreet questioning. "I hope that I can see Juanito later on the beach," she said, taking a sip of her tea. "Unless your wife would object."

"Why should she?" Jorge was extracting a cigarette from a package in his breast pocket. "You don't mind if I smoke?"

"No, of course not." Toni waited for her salad to be placed in front of her. "You've already finished your lunch?"

He made a graceful gesture of assent before using what appeared to be a solid gold lighter. "Juanito and I finished just a few minutes ago. My son would be pleased to see you on the beach later if you have time to bother with such things. Naturally, Juanito's still a little upset at being away from his mother." He leaned forward to deposit some ash in a ceramic tray on the table. "My wife lives in Puerto Rico. It's a matter of a trial separation at the moment. Perhaps later we will complete legal formalities. Since my position here is only temporary, it gives us a breathing space—if that is the right expression." His bemused tone showed that he knew very well it was the right expression.

Toni murmured a polite inanity, even as she gave the man full marks for his recital. In just a few words, he'd carefully put himself into the role of concerned father, misunderstood husband, and let her know that although there wasn't any chance of a future to their relationship, he'd be happy to further the acquaintance. It was just a pity, she thought, that he didn't apply for a United Nations job when he finished at Calabash. At the same time, she felt considerable sympathy for the absent Mrs. Benitez. Such glib assurance in a husband bespoke lots of practice in achieving his way—and with that profile, he'd probably spread his favors over a good part of the Caribbean. She'd have to ask Adam if the politically minded Rafael used the same tactics.

"You seem preoccupied, Miss Morgan. Or may I call you Antonia? Things are informal here at Calabash—it fits our way of life."

It was impossible to resist his courteous, almost courtly, approach. Toni showed no hesitation at all, saying, "Of course, Mr. Benitez. But most people call me Toni."

He nodded approvingly. "The name fits you. And please—since we are to be friends—will you call me

Jorge? Or, if you'd prefer, it can be George—the American equivalent."

"No." Toni bit her lip to hide her amusement. "Jorge is better. The name fits you," she repeated mischievously.

"So be it. Well, now that we have that settled"—he reached across to snub out his cigarette with a decisive gesture—"would you be free to spend part of the afternoon with me? Juanito's arrival has interrupted my work schedule already and the day is too beautiful to be ignored."

"I know what you mean. I was tossing a mental coin whether to explore the island or just go straight out to the beach and work on a suntan."

"You mean this is your first trip to St. John?"

"Fresh off the launch." Toni was glad that he hadn't been aboard that launch with Juanito to have watched her mad dash to the rail. "One of your newer guests."

His smile was a flash of white against his tanned skin. "Better and better. Then you must let me give you a short tour of the island. We have a social director who takes guests every morning but I do it in a much more comprehensive way."

"I'm sure of that." Toni's smile appeared in response to his teasing. "But what about Juanito?"

"There is no conflict. His nurse is with him and he probably will nap for most of the afternoon." Jorge snapped his fingers as if a thought had just occurred to him and he got to his feet. "But I must change and you probably will want to, as well."

"I would like to put on something else," she admitted.

"Then we can meet in the parking lot which is

down below at the back of this Tower. Shall we say forty-five minutes?" His gaze went to her half-eaten lunch. "Or is that enough time?"

"Fine, thank you."

"You're sure it's convenient? You had no other— commitments?"

There was no doubt about it, he should have been in the diplomatic service, Toni thought. For an instant she let herself wonder how Adam would like being called a "commitment." Then she smiled again and said blithely, "Not a one."

He picked up her hand and patted it in a way that made it impossible to take offense. No woman in her right mind would have even been tempted to. "Then I shall see you soon. I can't tell you how much I'm looking forward to it."

Her bungalow was still empty when Toni walked back to it and she felt a distinct twinge of disappointment that Adam wasn't around. She'd hoped that he might be impatiently waiting and she'd planned to announce her afternoon's schedule with calculated effect. It was considerably less satisfying to simply change into a cotton skirt and blouse in an empty set of rooms, with only the soft sound of breakers on the beach for company.

She lingered by the desk, wondering whether she should leave a note in time-honored fashion, when a soft knock came at the door, followed almost immediately by the rasp of a key in the lock. A uniformed maintenance man came in an instant later, pail in hand.

"Sorry, ma'am," he said, pulling up just over the threshold. "I didn't think there was anybody in this bungalow yet. Reception didn't let me know."

"That's all right—there's no harm done." She eyed the pail and then remembered Adam's earlier words. "Do you bring the ice each day?"

"Yes, ma'am. Is it all right to fill the buckets now?"

"Of course. Just close the door when you're finished, will you?"

"Yes, ma'am. I always do," he said with some resignation.

There was no answer she could make to that so she simply nodded. As she picked up a sweater to put around her shoulders, she decided against leaving a note for Adam. There'd be time enough to tell him of her progress when she returned.

The guests at Calabash must either have been secluded in their rooms or were enjoying the sunshine on the beaches because the expanse of green lawn was deserted as Toni cut across it toward the Tower and adjacent parking lot. She located the shuttle bus stop for later forays but didn't encounter a living creature except for one of the little brown weasel-like creatures that Juanito had admired earlier. This time, the rodent was darting around the trunk of a spectacular flamboyant tree, intent on increasing the distance between them, so Toni wasn't able to get a good look.

He was still on her mind when she reached the dusty parking lot on the far side of the Tower a minute or so later and saw Jorge waiting by the door of a small blue sedan.

"I like a woman who remembers to look at her watch," he said with another flashing smile as he opened the car door.

"It would be terrible to keep anyone waiting in

this heat." She lingered before she got in. "Before I forget, tell me about those little brown animals on the grounds here. The ones with the fuzzy tails."

"You and Juanito." He shook his head in mock dismay. "He wanted to take one with him to his room. I told him, though, that a mongoose isn't a good pet."

"A mongoose! Good Lord!" Toni looked thoughtful as she got in the car and let him close the door behind her. When he came around and slid behind the steering wheel, she said, "I thought they lived in jungles fighting snakes or in Rudyard Kipling stories. I never expected to see one face to face. Not that it was exactly face to face," she amended, "it was really the other end."

"Be thankful for that," Jorge said, as he drove through a back gate of the resort, giving a casual salute to the uniformed guard who waved them past. "Sometimes they get a little too close for comfort."

"You mean they're dangerous?"

He shrugged. "They're inquisitive animals and they've been known to invade the bungalows. It's a good idea to keep the porch doors closed. Not that they're really dangerous," he added with a sideways glance at Toni's still figure. "Just a little disconcerting in the middle of the night."

"How big do they get?"

"About two feet if they're fully grown. The ones I've seen on the lawns at Calabash are much smaller."

"I'll be sure to keep my sliding door closed. As a matter of fact, I'm sorry that I asked. Is there anything else I should be worrying about?"

"I should think the two-legged species at Calabash is a greater threat," he said, as they reached the end of the curving drive and turned onto a slightly wider two-laned road which went around the thickly forested hillside. "Naturally I'm referring to some of our guests—not the paid staff."

She noted his dry humor with relief and sat back to enjoy the ride. Thank heaven, he didn't feel compelled to make romantic overtures just to keep his hand in. "I'm glad of that," she said lightly. "I just want to relax and enjoy these gorgeous surroundings." She gestured toward the luxuriant vegetation. "So far I haven't recognized a single tree except the palms."

"This is one of the few orchards left on the island—soursops, sugar apples, a few limes, and guavas. You see, after sugar production collapsed on St. John, most of the land was simply used for pasture."

Toni stared as they passed a herd of goats grazing with a cow at the roadside. "The farmers seem pretty casual about their livestock."

"People on St. John like it that way. They've had a violent history of slavery and revolt. Today they're striving for a peaceful way of life with an independent voice in the future. And determined to get it—one way or another."

Toni risked a thoughtful glance at Jorge's profile. His voice had been devoid of expression but there was no doubt that he was mouthing Rafael's proclamations about the political future of the Caribbean.

Her silence must have had an effect on the man at her side because his tone was almost sheepish as he went on. "Naturally, all this can be achieved without leaving the livestock to run free. I must admit I would prefer that the farmers around here erected some fences. It's dangerous to drive this road at night with the animals wandering around. Dangerous for both parties."

"It would be worse if I was driving. I'd never remember to stay on the left. Especially since we're in the American Virgin Islands."

He shrugged. "It's custom that counts here. Fortunately the farm animals don't present much of a hazard further on. This highway goes along the mountain spine but later we'll drop down to the beach area where most people congregate. The tourists don't waste time driving around while they're on the island."

"You mean they're swimming instead?" When he nodded, she asked wistfully, "Can we see the famous underwater park?"

"Of course—if you're thinking of Trunk Bay and the publicized underwater trail. Do you want to go snorkeling?"

"I'm not really dressed for it."

He took his attention from the narrow curving road long enough for a thorough appraisal. "I thought maybe there was a bikini under your outfit. It's hard to tell without asking. Some of the swimsuits I've seen at Calabash could fit in the pocket of that blouse of yours."

"Mine fits in a beach bag along with a towel," Toni told him. "And right now, it's in my suitcase back at the bungalow."

"Then we'll simply take a look at Trunk Bay as we drive by and visit the Annaberg Ruins instead. No one could object to a program like that."

"I didn't mean that I was objecting . . ." She broke off as she saw his thin lips curve upward. Instead of adding to his amusement with her denials, she said, "Tell me about the ruin."

"It once was an old sugar mill. There's not much to be seen but there is a marvelous view across to the British Virgins. We can sit on what's left of the old wall and enjoy a cold drink while we look at our island chain."

After that, there was little more conversation as he drove the small car competently along the central highway, treating the hairpin curves with casual disregard. Occasionally they'd meet hikers on the roadside or pass one of the jeeplike open-air taxis crammed with well-tanned young people.

"From Cinnamon Bay probably," Jorge said after having to follow a taxi for a considerable distance because there wasn't a safe place to pass.

"Is that another resort like Calabash?"

"Hardly in the same league. Cinnamon Bay is a public campground." His tone made it sound almost indecent.

Toni nearly commented that the people looked as if they were having a wonderful time despite the difference in room rates. Instead she kept her expression bland to preserve the harmony between them.

"Ah—now we can be on our way," Jorge said in some relief as the jeep pulled over on the shoulder to let them get past. He waved his hand in acknowledgment as he accelerated, turning off the main road a little farther down by a sign that said "Annaberg Ruins."

There was still heavy vegetation on either side of the track and Jorge gestured toward a tree with unusual round fruit on its spindly branches. "Our namesake," he said, slackening speed. Seeing Toni's puzzled face, he added, "The calabash tree. Up ahead to the right is a tamarind. If we hadn't brought our own refreshment, we could brew tea from its seed pods."

"I'll remember. What's that strange-looking one with the red paint on it?" She craned to peer at it as he shifted onto a gravel side road leading up a steep hillside. "There's another one of the same kind."

"And both of them are to be avoided." He accelerated, and gravel came up against the fenders on the rough road. "That red paint is used as a warning. It's a manchineel tree."

"I still don't see . . ."

He shot her an impatient look. "Surely you've heard of them? But no—I should have remembered. They're not in the States. Unfortunately there are a great many in the Caribbean. Columbus called their small green fruit-'death apples.' "

"You've convinced me." She raised her hand in a fervent oath. "No small green apples this trip."

"The catch is—one doesn't have to eat the fruit. There's a dangerous sap in the leaves and bark, as well. You can be injured badly if any part of the manchineel is touched."

"And I thought I suffered when I hung my washcloth on a poison-oak bush at summer camp years ago."

"Believe me, this would be much worse."

"It certainly sounds like it." As they drove into a parking area below a remnant of the old stone wind-mill tower and Jorge braked, she said, "Maybe we should just have a cold drink in the car."

He laughed and proceeded to turn off the ignition.

"My dear Toni, your National Park Service is taking good care of you. There are no poisonous trees here in the ruins. Come." He opened the door and got out, reaching behind his seat to extract a padded bag. "We will go up and sit on the wall so you can admire our scenery. Possibly a small ant may come along, but I promise you, nothing fiercer."

Toni grinned sheepishly and let herself be persuaded. She made sure a little later, however, that there were no red-painted tree trunks within sight when they sat down on the waist-high stone wall which surrounded the old cane plantation and drank iced tea from a flask.

It would have been hard to find a prettier spot. Two flamboyant trees covered with red blooms provided shade on either side and even the rocky soil at their feet boasted a thin carpet of green grass which extended to the old stone tower nearby. Down below their hillside, the trees were thick and the vegetation was a rich variety of green. When it came to the sea stretched in front of them, it was as if all those shades of green had been diluted and changed to create a marvelous spectrum of blue. The patch reefs with the shallower water showed lighter shades as did the fringing reefs adjacent to the steep shore. In between, the deeper water took on dark jewel tones which were unrelieved except where white marked the channels of prevailing waves.

The island forms themselves were identical in coloring but their fingerlike peninsulas provided an enchanting variety of cover while the steep headlands shadowed a flotilla of sailboats passing beneath them.

Toni stared in silent contentment at the scene as

she sipped her tea, scarcely able to believe that anything could be so beautiful.

Jorge made no attempt to disturb her until he'd finished his drink and reached for a cigarette. "You look like someone who's been given a special present," he said then. "Now do you understand why St. John is so popular?"

Toni started to gesture and then her hand dropped to her side. "There aren't enough adjectives. I've never seen anything like it."

"And yet you're sitting on the site of an old slave village. I doubt if those poor devils found it so fine when they looked over this same wall." He drained the last drops of tea onto the ground and replaced his glass in the padded bag before looking up to meet her gaze. "Maybe the poet Housman was thinking of them when he wrote of his 'voice of tears—that wept of old the endless ill.'"

"I imagine there were plenty of horrors a lot closer to home." She finished her own tea and handed the glass back to him. "I refuse to let past misery spoil the present for us. Especially on such a pretty afternoon."

"You're right, of course." The man beside her flushed and savagely ground his almost-untouched cigarette into the top of the wall before he threw it down into the dense vegetation beneath. Then his mouth twisted into a wry smile. "Actually, you're very good for me, Toni. I have been alone too much these past few weeks. It has been difficult"—he hesitated perceptibly over the last word—"without my wife."

"You said she was in Puerto Rico?" Toni probed delicately.

"That's right." He picked up her hand and played absently with her fingers. "I haven't been in contact with her at all since I agreed to fill in temporarily here at Calabash. I felt I needed time to think."

"Were you in the hotel business in Puerto Rico, too?"

"My family owns two hotels in San Juan." There was an unconscious undertone of hauteur to his deep voice, all Latin American male. "I have been trained in every part of the operation. Lately though, I've wondered if I've chosen the wrong career."

Toni kept her voice light, "I think that's about par for the course."

His eyebrows drew together. "You mean it?"

"About waffling over a career? Of course. Everyone does it."

Jorge's perplexed reaction showed that this aspect had never occurred to him. Probably, Toni thought in resignation, he'd been so adamant in ruling his family roost that nobody dared tell him it wasn't a sin to change his mind. Or was it? Suddenly it occurred to her that Rafael Benitez might have been responsible for his brother's recent change of heart. Could it be that the family hotel business was too tame when the younger brother was lighting torches of revolt all around the Caribbean?

"At least, it will be nice for you to be with your son again," she said, changing the subject after looking at her watch. "And speaking of Juanito, his nap must be over by now. We should be getting back."

Jorge shrugged and brought her fingers up to his lips in a graceful gesture before releasing her hand.

"It would be nicer to stay here with you and watch the sunset over the water. Just the two of us."

Toni got to her feet so that he wouldn't be tempted to pursue that idea. Her watch had shown that it was much later than she'd dreamed. For the first time, she was regretting that she hadn't left a note for Adam. He might be sticking a few pins of his own in her voodoo doll at that very moment.

Her foot slipped on a rock as she turned to start back down the hill toward the car and the twinge of pain in her ankle made her grin ruefully. Maybe her fantasies weren't so far off, after all.

"You look as if the idea wouldn't displease you," Jorge persisted, taking his time about following her.

Toni turned and glanced over her shoulder at him. "What idea? Oh, you mean staying here. Unfortunately reality raises its ugly head. That's another cliché for saying duty calls."

"But you're on vacation. You told me that there was no reason you couldn't take the afternoon off."

"I've taken it." She kept her words light as she picked her way down the rocky trail which led back to the parking area and the car. "We'll be lucky to be back in time for dinner."

He waved that aside as they neared the car. "There is plenty of time. I can arrange to have dinner served to us at any hour."

"Oh, but I really can't . . ."

He looked up from unlocking the door, a frown on his face. "You can't join me for dinner? But I thought you wanted to see my son again. Naturally he won't eat with us but there will be time for a short visit." Jorge had opened the door for her but he didn't stand aside, so there was no way she could get in without forcibly pushing him out of the way. For an instant Toni had visions of being left to hitch a ride all the way back to Calabash.

"I can't promise," she said. "First of all, I'll have to check with Mr. Driscoll."

"And exactly who is this Mr. Driscoll?" he asked in a steely tone.

"A man I know. I sort of—work—for him."

"What does that have to do with our plans for dinner?"

"I have to see if he approves," Toni admitted, wishing that Jorge wouldn't turn a simple afternoon drive into a minor Spanish Inquisition. A bright yellow bananaquit soared past, headed for the branches of a nearby tree, and Toni yearned suddenly for the bird's freedom.

"I'd thought that I'd finally discovered a woman who had established the proper priorities of life," Jorge was going on angrily. "Now I find that you're simply another female who's content to exist with a man who pays well. At least I trust he pays you well. The fact that he's accommodated you at Calabash shows that you must have talents above the ordinary."

Toni drew herself up. "I'd like to think so. Now, will you take me back, please."

"What's the hurry?" Jorge's hands came down heavily on her shoulders and he pulled her against his shirtfront. "Since I know how you operate—we might as well find enjoyment together."

Toni shoved back hard, trying to put a prudent distance between them. "Don't be ridiculous. I didn't come here for anything like that. Besides," she added, trying to think of a clinching argument, "Adam would have a fit."

He pulled her back tight against him, letting his thumbs press hard into her shoulder muscles. "*Dios!* As if I cared what this Adam thinks—" His head bent determinedly to capture her lips, but when he was just a breath away he jerked upward again. "Did you say Adam? Adam Driscoll?"

Toni swallowed and tried to control her panicky breathing. "That's right. I didn't leave a note for him, so he'll be really upset."

"*Callete!*" He enforced his command to be silent with a brutal shake which made her head bob painfully. "I must think."

Toni would like to have retaliated but there was a smoldering anger about him that made her hesitate to try anything. Until that moment, she hadn't realized that any man could react so violently to such a simple announcement. He still had a tight grip on her but she managed to move away from the car so that there'd be a chance of escape in case she could get free. Not that she'd have a prayer if Jorge really lost his temper and came after her. She gave an involuntary shudder at the thought, vowing that if she ever got back to Calabash, she wouldn't put a toe outside the screen without a bodyguard.

"I take it that you're living with this man . . ."

Benitez' cold utterance brought her abruptly back to reality.

Her own voice matched his for frigidity. "I *work* for Mr. Driscoll. We're merely sharing a bungalow because there wasn't any other space available."

"Spare me the platitudes." His accent had deepened. "You could have told me before."

"I wasn't trying to hide anything. All you had to do was check with the reception clerk."

"I told you—I was at the other end of the island picking up my son." His handsome features suddenly looked tired in the late-afternoon light. "We were expecting Mr. Driscoll. Somehow I did not expect you to be associated with such a man." He gestured almost wearily toward the front seat of the car. "Get in. It's time we were going."

Toni's expression was wary but she knew that she had no choice but to obey him. There still wasn't a soul to be seen in the old ruins, so there was no help to be had from an unexpected quarter. She could only hope that Jorge's anger had passed and wouldn't flare again. Certainly he appeared more resigned to the situation by then.

When he'd gotten in the car beside her and started the engine, she said tentatively, "I don't know why you're so down on Mr. Driscoll. The feeling certainly isn't shared by the owners of Calabash—" She broke off at the sound of a car approaching when they reached the park turnoff beyond the ominous red-painted trees.

A small pickup came over the hill and braked just enough to take the road to the ruins, sending a shower of gravel as the tires skidded in the turn.

"You were saying something about Driscoll?" Jorge's voice sounded flat as they pulled out onto the coastal road and headed back toward the resort. When Toni didn't reply, he frowned and bestowed a suspicious glance on her. "What's the matter? Have you run out of praise for your 'employer'? It's all right—you needn't worry that I'll tell him about what happened this afternoon."

Toni opened her mouth to protest and then closed her lips again, pressing them tight together to keep them from trembling. She tried to ignore the memory of his angry face so close to hers and thanked heaven that the kiss had never landed. Even without it, her reaction was bad enough. And that was before the pickup truck had appeared on the scene. It had only taken a glimpse of the bearded driver to make her stomach muscles tighten even more. The man who had been with Rafael Benitez in New Orleans and later in Puerto Rico had managed to arrive in St. John. And there was no doubt in her mind that trouble—real trouble—wouldn't be far behind.

Chapter Seven

It was fortunate Toni didn't realize that events would get even worse before they got better.

There was certainly no way of foretelling that they would be held up by a mudslide which blocked the road just a few miles further down. Along with two or three other cars, they were forced to wait until the maintenance crew shoveled the debris aside. When Toni asked tentatively if there weren't an alternate route, Jorge had muttered that it would take longer than staying where they were. After that, Toni hadn't asked any more questions and he had remained broodingly silent behind the wheel.

By the time they reached Calabash, the soft tropical dusk was settling. Jorge parked in the lot behind the Tower, where the sound of dinner music could be heard as it floated across the still air from the dining area by the beach.

It would have been ridiculous to thank Jorge for a pleasant afternoon, but Toni managed something innocuous and saw him jerk his head in response before she hurried out of the lot. Discreet lights along the path crossing the lawn made it easy to follow and she had plenty of time to wish that she'd spent the afternoon at the resort rather than going out with the

Calabash manager. Only the knowledge that she'd acquired about the Benitez family and that glimpse of the bearded man made her feel a little better about the whole thing.

As she fumbled for her key at the bungalow, she hoped fervently that Adam would look at her escapade in the same way.

The door knob was yanked from her grasp as she opened it and it only took one glance at Adam's seething face for Toni to realize there was no hope in that direction either.

"Where in the bloody hell have you been?" he ground out before she could even step across the threshold. "I was about to call the Coast Guard and Park Rangers to look for your remains."

Toni pushed by him wearily and dropped her purse onto the closest table. "Well, it isn't necessary. I'm sorry if I spoiled your fun."

At that, he yanked her back against him. His hands bit into her shoulders to administer a sharp shake—stopping abruptly as she gasped in pain and almost sagged at his feet.

"What the devil's the matter?" He shifted his hands to lead her across to an armchair and pushed her down into it. "You look like something the tide washed in. What happened?"

"I'm just a little tender there," she said, rubbing the bruised skin on her shoulders. "Jorge did the same thing to me. A woman needs a suit of armor these days."

He sensibly ignored the last remark, honing in on the others with grim determination. "Who's Jorge? What do you mean—did the same thing? Has somebody been bothering you? Tell me!"

"I'm trying to." She bit her lip as he hovered angrily above her. "Don't look like that. As if you were going to . . ."

"Murder somebody?" For the first time since she'd come in the room, his expression softened to normal lines. "I think I passed that point about an hour ago. Since then I've been trying to decide whether to use boiling oil or thumbscrews on you. But the way you look"—his stern mouth softened even more to approach a slanted grin—"I think you've suffered enough. Now tell me—who the hell is Jorge?"

Toni waved him down into the other chair and started to explain. By the time she mentioned seeing Rafael's bearded follower at the plantation ruins, the scowl was back on Adam's face. "Jorge didn't let on that he knew him, though," she finished. "Of course, he was still annoyed at that point about my connection with you." She shuddered at the memory. "He made me feel as if I should be paraded through the town streets. I don't know whether it was because he thought I was a . . ."

"Fallen woman?"

She nodded. "Or whether it was because you're paying the rent. He really dislikes you. Are you sure that you've never met him or his wife?"

"I'm sure. Good Lord, you make it sound as if I'd been responsible for their separation."

"I didn't mean to." Toni rubbed her forehead with unsteady fingers. "But why should he be so unreasonable?"

"Who knows? Maybe he really fancied you and doesn't like competition. Or maybe brother Rafael has gotten to him about deciding future Calabash policy. We'll find out eventually. Now, I'd better see if I can find you some dinner. You don't look up to sitting through soup to nuts in the main dining room and I'm afraid it's too late for the others. With any luck, I can wangle a tray for room service."

"Can't I just phone?" Toni grimaced then as she remembered that telephones were an endangered species at Calabash. "Damn!"

"I know. You're talking to a man who spent most of the afternoon at a pay phone by the bar. The musicians rehearse in a room right next to it. It would have been easier if I'd sent a message to the mainland in a bottle."

No wonder he looked tired, Toni thought. All the hassle about what was going to happen at Calabash plus the worry she'd unwittingly provided. "Did you manage some dinner?" she asked meekly.

"Enough. I waited for a while and then decided that you must have gone to one of the other dining rooms." He frowned at his watch and stood up. "If I don't get going, the kitchen will be closed for sure."

The door closed behind him and Toni heard him go down the outside stone steps two at a time. As she got to her feet, her glance moved to the full-length mirror on the back of the closet door, where it stopped in dismay. No wonder that Adam had left in such haste. Considering the way she looked, it was surprising that he'd let her in the bungalow at all. She unbuttoned her blouse as she headed for the shower and then paused, finally detouring by her open suitcase to get her swimsuit. A quick dip in the ocean would accomplish the same thing as a shower and it would probably be a lot more fun.

She hurriedly changed into her suit and pulled on a nylon beach skirt, finally grabbing a bath towel from the rack before letting herself out the sliding glass door. As she stepped out onto the front porch, the early nighttime air caressed her skin, making it unnecessary to drape the towel around her shoulders as she walked to the beach.

There was enough moonlight so that any other illumination was unnecessary and Toni felt a thrill of anticipation as she deserted the path to scuff through the sand when she reached the low stone wall edging the beach proper. She wasn't alone in her decision to enjoy an evening swim but the only other guests were out on the jetty near the reception area. Toni stopped by a plastic lounger long enough to take off her nylon skirt and toss the towel down beside it. An instant later, she was running into the gently curling waves.

The warm saltwater closed around her like a silken sheath and she turned on her back, letting the buoyancy support her. Down the beach, the sound of music coming from the lounge mingled with the even metronome of waves hitting the shore. An occasional shriek of feminine laughter was evidence that the bar where the musicians were playing was doing a rousing business. That made her recall Adam's comment about making himself heard over the afternoon rehearsal and she decided to get back to the bungalow before he returned. She stroked toward the shore, trying to keep her hair dry. That way, she'd look halfway decent for the rest of the evening.

She waded out of the water reluctantly, but told herself that the beach wouldn't disappear like an illusion. Adam might even join her in a midnight swim after she'd eaten.

That promising thought caused her to pull on an attractive pair of lounging pajamas in pale peony pink when she returned to the cottage. A knock on the door just as she'd finished applying a matching lipstick made her frown. Her forehead smoothed when she decided that Adam had simply neglected to take a key in his haste.

Opening the door wide a minute later, she was stricken to see a tall uniformed waiter bearing a tray on his shoulder.

"Your dinner, ma'am." He strode in to deposit it on the table beside one of the easy chairs and brought a slip back for her to sign. "Mr. Driscoll said to tell you he'd be along shortly but to go ahead and eat. Something about having to see a man or maybe he had to drive to Cruz Bay—I don't remember for sure."

"That's all right." Toni tried to sound as if she'd expected this latest setback when she signed the slip and returned it to him. "Exactly where is Cruz Bay?"

"Just at the end of the island. Not far." He whisked the plastic covers from the dishes and stacked them neatly to one side. "Enjoy your food, ma'am. When you're finished, just put the tray outside on the porch. Somebody will collect it."

When he'd gone, Toni surveyed the plate of fried chicken dispassionately, finally picking up a leg to nibble on it. The first taste made her realize that she was hungrier than she'd thought and she attacked the accompanying salad and rolls with enthusiasm. There was even coffee which tasted good although it wasn't very hot. She prudently left some in the insulated carafe, thinking that Adam might appreciate it when he finally arrived.

She tried not to watch the clock but it must have been almost an hour before she heard footsteps on the porch and the welcome sound of his key in the lock.

He appeared surprised to find her sitting in one of the easy chairs, with an open magazine in her lap. "Still up? I thought you'd have called it quits by now," he said, going over to toss his key on the bureau and take off his sports coat, putting it in the closet. "My God, I'm tired." The last came as he moved over beside her and peered into the dish that had held the fried chicken. "Anything edible left?"

"Not unless you and Dracula are soul-mates."

"I see what you mean." He picked up the solitary chicken neck and then put it down again. "Not tonight."

"There *is* some coffee." She gestured toward the carafe, thinking it would be nice if he mentioned that her lounging outfit was a great improvement over what he'd seen before. When he didn't, her tone sharpened. "We'll have to try and have a meal together—just for the novelty. Maybe sometime before we leave."

He tugged at his collar, grimacing as if it had shrunk suddenly. "I'm sorry—something came up. I'll take a cup of that coffee but let me get rid of this tie first." He gave her a crooked smile over his shoulder as he moved toward the bureau again. "You have the right idea. That pajama thing you're wearing looks comfortable."

Toni had a vision of the French designer choking violently if he'd heard an adjective like "comfortable" applied to his creation but she didn't let on. She sat quietly, sipping her own coffee as she watched Adam pull off his necktie and unbutton the collar of his shirt before coming back to sit across from her. He drained the coffee into an extra cup and leaned back to drink it, stretching his long legs out with a sigh.

"The waiter said you had to meet a man," she prompted when the silence lengthened.

"That's what I told him. Actually I wanted to do some more telephoning but this time I thought I'd better not use the phones here. The situation's getting worse—the latest is that the help is planning a general strike late tomorrow. Apparently Calabash is the first target. Afterwards, it could spread to the rest of the island. Maybe even to St. Thomas and St. Croix."

"I gather that Rafael's been busy."

"He supplies the kindling—then someone else lights the fire. The worst part is," Adam continued, leaning forward to emphasize his point, "there are rumors of more violence to come. Rafael is a great believer in getting his point over."

"What can you do?"

"A couple of Calabash directors are flying in tomorrow morning. They've scheduled a meeting with the top locals afterwards." Adam drained his coffee and put the empty cup on the tray, getting restlessly to his feet. "I left word for your friend Jorge that Calabash's manager will be expected to be there, too."

"He's not my friend and not yours either," she reminded him.

"I know. That's why I'm not putting any money on this meeting being a success." Adam rubbed his face wearily. "It's a lot easier to shout and threaten than to indulge in constructive negotiation. Well, I'm going to bed." As if his conscience had suddenly nudged him, he added, "It hasn't been much fun for you, has it? I'm sorry. When I asked you to come along—I didn't think it would turn out like this."

His apologetic tone was so unlike his crisp assured one that Toni's eyes widened in surprise. Adam walked over to the bureau to retrieve his tie, as he said, "If it's all right with you, I'll borrow the bathroom first for a shower—then I'll be out of your way." His eyes surveyed the sliding vinyl curtain nearby. "You need any help with that thing?"

Almost as if he couldn't wait to pull it and get her out of his sight, Toni thought indignantly. Aloud she said, "No, I can manage. I'll do it last thing."

He shrugged. "Whatever you want."

Toni opened her magazine again as he walked to his suitcase to pull out pajamas and a dark green silk robe. The muscles in his back rippled under the thin fabric of his shirt as he bent over and rummaged in the case, making Toni more aware than ever of his leashed masculine strength. Not that she'd reason to doubt it; she still could feel the way his lean fingers had fastened on her earlier. If only he'd use that strength for something constructive, she thought idly, like taking her in his arms and using those hands to explore every . . .

Suddenly she realized the way her thoughts were leading and blood rushed to her cheeks.

"I'll get a move on then."

She became aware that Adam had spoken and raised her gaze to meet his puzzled one. "I'm sorry," she said, confused. "I was thinking of something else."

He cut her off with a brusque gesture. "It wasn't important." Then, peering at her more closely, "You're sure you feel all right?"

"I feel fine."

His eyebrows went up slightly at her tone and he opened his mouth as if to dispute it before discretion triumphed. He abruptly disappeared in the bathroom, closing the door behind him with more emphasis than needed.

Toni tossed her magazine on the table, and matched Adam's restrained violence as she piled the china on their supper tray. She looked around, unsure of what to do with it when she was finished, and then remembered the waiter's suggestion. Choosing the front porch because it was nearer, she shouldered the sliding glass door open and deposited the tray outside. Afterwards, she absently pulled the door back as she heard water being turned on full force in the shower.

That spurred her to pull the vinyl room separator partway across the room on its metal track so that when Adam emerged he'd see that she was anxious for separate quarters as well. Then she put her palms up to cool her flushed cheeks so that her appearance would be equally convincing. Thank heaven, he hadn't been able to read her mind during their last exchange! Toni shook her head vexedly as she thought about it. The way she was behaving, *she* should be the one taking a cold shower.

What a time to realize that Adam held more than casual attraction; that all the verbal sparring on her part had been purely a defense against her true instincts. It was easier that way because if she'd come right out and faced reality, she would have allied herself with the other women who'd crossed his path and been discarded when their attraction waned. Adam had acted like the typical male in refusing to mention any past involvement but with Nora for a roommate, Toni had learned a great deal about his prowess with the feminine sex. In New Orleans she'd doubted his avowal to keep things on a businesslike basis when they traveled together. What irony to discover now that *she* was the one regretting the status quo!

She moved over to stare out at the moonlit beach, aware that she'd have to be more careful than ever to keep her feelings hidden. Damned if the man would have the chance to hang another scalp on his belt!

If Adam noticed her subdued manner when he emerged from the bath a few minutes later, he was wary enough not to comment on it. He just clinched the belt of his robe a little tighter and said, "The bath's all yours. I used the rack on the back of the door for my towels—you can have the rest of the space."

Toni nodded, keeping her glance averted as she walked around the end of his bed where he'd dropped the damp towel he'd used to dry his hair. She was tempted to remind him that a wet sheet wouldn't improve his disposition but since he was combing his hair in front of the bureau by then, she decided against it. If she couldn't flirt with the man, she certainly wasn't going to start dispensing household hints like a maiden aunt!

When she came out of the bathroom five minutes later, Adam had gotten into bed and was reading the magazine she'd left on the table. He'd buttoned his dark green pajama coat and hitched the sheet discreetly up to his hips. The look he cast over the top of the magazine didn't miss an inch of her pale peach gown which she'd changed into or the thigh-length wrap jacket of matching material which she wore over it.

Toni met his glance with equal aplomb, mentally congratulating herself for her unhurried gait—just as if she'd spent half her life walking around men's bedrooms. And if Nora hadn't been talking out of turn, she might actually convince Adam of it.

"I thought you didn't bring any pajamas along on this trip," she accused suddenly, remembering his comment from the night before.

"I didn't. I bought these today at the resort shop to spare your tender feelings," he said, showing that her display of nonchalance hadn't convinced anybody.

"Oh." Her voice dropped for an instant along with her confidence. Sensibly then, she decided to change the subject. "I'll pull the curtain the rest of the way in just a second. After I get some ice for a glass of water, I'll leave you in peace."

"Take your time. I hadn't really planned to drop right off to sleep," Adam said laconically, lowering the magazine a little more. "As a matter of fact, feel free to walk around whenever you want. It won't disturb me."

"Well, I'll try not to set off any bombs or rockets before breakfast." Toni put her glass on the table by her double bed and lifted the lid of the ice bucket which was next to it. She peered down and announced, "I think that fellow forgot to bring his afternoon delivery—this is mostly chips and water."

Adam's head remained bent over his article. "Try the bucket in here if there isn't enough. Maybe the lack of service is part of a slowdown and the management forgot to tell us. Unless Jorge let something slip to your shell-like ears."

His sarcasm made Toni look up from her task of extracting half-melted cubes from the bucket. She was about to answer in kind when suddenly she heard a rustle on the floor close by. Automatically glancing down, her eyes caught a flash of brown on the carpet under the bed table and the next thing she knew, some tiny animal scurried over her bare instep. Her gasp of surprise broke off as she felt a distinctly stringy tail dragging across her skin.

In that instant, Toni did what any red-blooded woman would do. She opened her mouth and let out a terrorized shriek that rattled the pictures. In trying to escape up on the bed, away from feet and tails, she whacked the edge of the table with her knee and sent it flying. The lamp atop it crashed onto the edge of the mattress and slithered back down, denting the shade on the way. The bucket shot off the table top as fast as a rocket from Canaveral and landed on its side in the middle of the bed, depositing a swath of ice cubes and water on the mattress like fallout from an erupting volcano.

"What the hell!"

Toni heard Adam's exclamation from the other room as she reached the top of the bed. Her toes were already squishing in icy water when he arrived at the edge of her mattress seconds later. "God in heaven—have you lost your mind?" he wanted to know. Automatically, he rescued the lamp and moved it aside. "If you're trying to electrocute yourself, you're going about it in the right way," he added, straightening to put his hands on his hips. "I'd suggest getting down from there unless you plan to play in the water for the rest of the night."

Toni ignored that to ask nervously, "Is he gone?"

"Is who gone?" Adam's glance took in the empty room. "I don't see anybody."

"Look on the floor." Toni gathered the skirt of her nightgown tighter around her legs, trying to keep it out of the water. "I'm not getting down until that—thing—is gone."

"Okay, I'll bite. Animal, vegetable, or mineral?"

"Animal, of course," she snapped. "And I don't think it's funny. My feet are freezing."

"Allow me." He reached over to remove the two ice cubes which were resting against her heel before righting the table and replacing the bucket on it.

"Just see if it's gone," she pleaded, rubbing one foot against the other and almost falling off the bed in the process.

"Stand still or you'll break your neck! How big an animal?"

"I don't know. Maybe a mongoose. No, it couldn't have been. It didn't have a fuzzy tail like the one I saw on the lawn and I felt little feet. But it was brown—sort of like a—" Her voice trailed off.

"Mouse." There was resignation in his tone along with something else.

"Of course not!" she countered scornfully. "My Lord, I know a mouse when I see one."

"But you didn't see it," he pointed out. "You just felt it. Little feet and a tail that wasn't fuzzy."

She closed her eyes and shuddered, remembering. "It was stringy and it slithered. Right over the top of my foot." A muffled noise made her eyes flash open again as her gaze accusingly found Adam's. "If you're just going to stand around and laugh, you can leave any time."

"I thought you wanted me to look for the mouse."

"It *wasn't* a mouse—it was bigger. What are you doing over there?" she wanted to know as he prowled around the edge of the room and then lingered by the sliding glass door to survey something on the porch. Absently she noted that he hadn't bothered to stop for a robe when he'd come plunging to her rescue and she wondered if he was as cold in his pajamas as she was in her nightgown. The overhead light revealed the outlines of his broad shoulders as he moved and it occurred to her that the same thing might be happening to her silhouette. She pulled her kimono even tighter around her, unconsciously achieving just what she hoped to avoid. "Do you see anything out there?" she asked when he slid the door closed.

"Just the remains on your dinner tray. In these parts, that's as good as issuing an engraved invitation. When you left the door open, too"—he jerked his head toward the one he'd just closed—"I'm surprised you didn't collect a convention of furry friends."

"My God!" She retreated to the center of the mattress even though it meant standing on ice particles. "Do you think there are more?"

"After that scream, they're halfway to St. Thomas by now."

"Very funny." She frowned as she surveyed the floor. "Are you sure?"

"Since you're not going to be in here, I can't see what difference it makes." He put up his hand to help her down. "If it makes you feel better, we can pull the divider to close off this end of the room. I doubt if your intruder is big enough to drag it open. If he is, then I'll join you on the front lawn."

Toni stared stonily down at Adam from her perch, ignoring his proffered hand. "What do you mean— about my not being in here?"

"Use your head, woman." He gestured impatiently toward the sodden bedding. "You can't seriously plan to spend the rest of the night on *that?*" When she hesitated, he went on in decisive tones, "And don't get any ideas about my offering to take your place. No way."

Toni sighed and, this time, let him help her off the bed. "I didn't really think you would. And there's no hope of getting that mattress replaced before morning."

"If then."

She chose to ignore that cryptic statement and watched him pull the vinyl room divider completely across the width of the room behind them.

"Just in case there are any other uninvited callers lingering by the woodwork," Adam said, making sure the divider was firmly fastened. As he turned, he seemed amused to see her standing by the upholstered chairs. "Don't tell me you're planning to sleep in one of those for the night?"

Toni, who had been considering just that, decided not to struggle any longer. "Not really. I don't think I'd last more than an hour or two." She tried not to look at the expanse of the twin beds with their common headboard.

Adam nodded and got back in his bed, reaching for his magazine with an unhurried movement. "There's an extra blanket in the closet if you want one."

Toni wriggled her frozen toes and decided that she needed more drastic relief. "I'll have a hot shower to thaw out."

"Good idea. If you got the hem of that nightgown damp, you'd better change it."

"It'll be dry in a few minutes." Toni gathered the skirt around her as she headed toward the bath, annoyed that he didn't give her credit for any intelligence. Hopefully, he'd have turned off the light and gone to sleep by the time she emerged from the shower.

"What happened to your legs?"

She stopped, startled by his abrupt question. Then she looked down, half expecting to have turned blue. "What are you talking about?"

"It looks as if you'd gotten thoroughly bitten." He'd lowered the magazine and was staring accusingly at her ankles. "Were you on the beach?"

"Well, yes. For heaven's sake—what's wrong with that?"

"What time were you out there?"

"While you were getting the dinner tray. You sound like Perry Mason. It isn't a crime to go swimming at Calabash at night, is it?"

"Of course not." He sounded irritated again. "But if you'd read the brochure on the desk, it would have warned you about the sand fleas that generally come

out after four o'clock here. They don't attack everyone but ..."

He didn't say any more. He didn't have to. Toni
clenched her fists and managed to refrain from
scratching the spots around her ankles that suddenly
felt as if they were on fire. "I don't expect they'll
bother me at all," she announced as she continued
toward the bathroom.

"In case they do, there's a tube of stuff in with
my shaving gear. Help yourself." Adam settled down
behind his magazine again.

Toni closed the bathroom door behind her and
sagged against the wooden barricade. She was half
frozen, her nightgown was sodden at the hemline,
and her ankles suddenly felt as if they'd been
branded with a hot iron. Despite all that, she still
had to go out and calmly share a bed with a man who
didn't even try to contain his boredom when she
panicked over a mouse and offered insect repellent in
the same dispassionate vein.

She summoned her strength then and reached in to
turn on the shower. There wasn't any way of solving
the dilemma until morning and at the rate she was
going she wouldn't last until then.

Her mood improved somewhat when she'd stood
under the hot water. By the time she emerged, her
nylon nightgown was nearly dry and she thanked
providence for such small favors as she donned it
again. Unfortunately, the bites on her ankles hadn't
subsided at all and the salve Adam had offered turned
out to be a distinct pink shade, so there was no hope
of using it undetected. Desperation triumphed over
vanity and she slapped the medication on with a lavish hand, hoping to stop the itching. She sniffed the

tube delicately when she'd finished and thanked heaven again—this time that the repellent had a pleasant fragrance so she wouldn't have to worry about that aspect of the cure.

Smoothing a comb through her hair, she made a final check on her appearance before opening the door. She fit into the "clean and well-scrubbed" category but that was better than applying lipstick or light makeup. Adam would take one look at that and ask if she always went to bed decked out like a circus horse.

With any luck, she told herself, he'd be asleep when she emerged. To make sure that she wouldn't awaken him, she carefully turned off the bathroom light before opening the door.

"Feel better?" Adam had never sounded more wide awake. He put down the magazine on the bedside table near his elbow and favored her with a deliberate masculine appraisal that took in everything between her still-damp hair and her bare toes. If he was impressed by any of her measurements in between, his features didn't show it. "I brought out the extra blanket," he said, gesturing to the bed alongside his where a white wool cover had been carefully spread over the upper sheet. "Usually a blanket's the last thing anybody needs here, but, of course..."

"... most people don't splash around in ice cubes before going to bed," Toni said, finishing it for him. She looked about her, wondering if there was any way she could stall—to avoid getting into that bed under his thoughtful stare. All of her books were still in her suitcase behind the vinyl curtain, so reading was out as an excuse. Besides, she'd revert to freezing again if she sat around under the revolving ceiling fans clad simply in her thin gown.

Adam must have sensed her dilemma because he suddenly yawned and made a production of shifting in his bed, shoving his pillow into a more comfortable position and reaching over to turn off his bedlamp. "Switch off the overhead light when you're finished," he told her, sliding down and pulling the sheet up over his shoulder with his usual economy of gesture. "And don't worry about setting an alarm—I'll wake up in plenty of time."

Time for what, Toni wanted to ask, letting her mind wander giddily over the prospects offered. Fortunately she had enough presence of mind not to dwell on such vagaries, going over instead to switch on her bed light before turning off the ceiling fixture.

The muted illumination added to the intimacy of the room and Toni kept her expression casual as she walked back to her side of the bed. For an instant she wondered whether to keep her kimono on and then decided not to add to Adam's amusement by such an infantile gesture. She compromised by switching off her bedlight and then, shrugging quickly out of the kimono, tossed it to the foot of the bed. The warmth of the wool blanket felt wonderful as she slid between the sheets and she pulled it up around her shoulders as she stretched out gingerly on the outer edge of her mattress. When her heartbeat settled back to its usual cadence, she discovered the moonlight filtering through the curtains was enough to serve as an unplanned nightlight. She turned her head carefully on the pillow and saw that Adam was also on the far edge of his mattress with his back to her. Almost as if proclaiming silently that he had no possible interest in anything within reach.

"Good night, Toni."

He didn't move a muscle but his dry comment showed he either had eyes in the back of his head or he knew how a woman's mind worked when she was in bed with him. There was no way he could have missed Toni's guilty start of surprise or the rustle she made when she hastily turned back on the pillow.

"I said good night," he persisted a second or so later. "You can't be asleep already."

"Of course not." Her tone was just as emphatic. "I was thinking of something else."

"If you're planning to have nightmares about that experience of yours in the other room, wait until morning. Another scream like the last one and the security men will come pounding on the door."

She heard him move then, thumping his pillow impatiently as he shifted on the mattress, but she kept her eyes focused on her side of the room. "If you must know, I was trying to keep from scratching my ankles," she fibbed.

"You're lucky to get off with a few insect bites. Next time read the resort brochure." When a telling silence greeted that comment, he muttered something and turned his back, pulling their shared spread with him.

Toni felt a sudden draft of cold air on her toes and opened her lips to protest vigorously. Just as quickly she closed them again. By then, she was so nervous trying to appear calm that she couldn't have kept her voice steady if she'd tried. And if she turned on the light to remake the bed, Adam would know the effect his pajama-clad body was having on her.

Toni carefully pulled up her legs until she found some covers again and kept a death grip on the top of the blanket so Adam couldn't divest her of that when he thrashed around the next time.

The minutes ticked noisily by on the wind-up travel clock at her ear, and she finally decided that she needn't have worried about any more movement from the man beside her. Adam stayed wrapped in his cocoon of bedding, acting much like the mummy his appearance suggested. His breathing was almost imperceptible, Toni found as she strained to hear. Even the gentle lap of the waves from the beach sounded more distinct. Surely it wasn't normal for anybody to sleep so quietly, and then she realized that he could be thinking exactly the same thing about her. Which could mean that he wasn't having any luck ignoring an unexpected bed partner either.

That possibility was so cheering that she relaxed for the first time and almost immediately fell sound asleep, her fingers still clutching the blanket.

When she awoke some hours later, she had no idea of the time. She *did* know that she was feeling as cold as the ice cubes she'd been standing in hours before. Her hand went out to search for the elusive blanket only to discover that it had somehow slithered across to the other mattress.

Which wasn't surprising, she decided, as she surveyed the situation. In the intervening hours, both she and Adam had gravitated to the center of the big bed. He still slept soundly beside her, hogging fully three-fourths of the blanket. She reached out tentative fingers to see if she could pull it from him. Adam responded with a protesting noise in his throat which stilled her hand immediately. Then she drew an exasperated breath as he settled even more comfortably under the warm cover.

Toni shivered in the cool air and decided to be practical. Unless she woke him by yanking the blanket away, there was only one alternative. She slid her pillow across to get as close as she dared without actually touching him and carefully pulled the remaining flap of blanket over her.

It was even better than she dared hope. She relaxed in his body warmth after she found that he continued to sleep peacefully. Toni kept her distance, although it had shrunk to two or three inches instead of the width of the mattress, and wondered why she had been so concerned earlier. At that moment, she was more than half asleep and decided to postpone such thoughts until morning. An instant later, her eyelids came down and stayed there.

The next time she surfaced to reality, the long, curtained windows of the room had something considerably brighter than moonlight behind them. Toni was reluctant to change position, and she stretched luxuriously before turning to check the bedside clock.

Her movement brought her up against a cool thigh and she froze instantly, her eyes widening in shocked surprise. She found herself staring into Adam's relaxed face as he slept, just inches away on the same pillow. Dim memories of her nocturnal wanderings in a search for the blanket surfaced then and Toni's cheeks flamed as she realized that she certainly possessed the major share of it. Adam's long pajama-clad body was only covered by the sheet from the knees down. The deprivation didn't appear to bother him; one of his arms was stretched alongside her hips and the other rested comfortably over her breast. Toni became aware of the warmth of his fingers through the thin fabric of her gown almost at the same instant Adam moved and opened his eyes.

As he became conscious of her nearness, his gaze narrowed and darkened, but other than that, he didn't make the slightest outward move. Toni drew in a tremulous breath as she stared back at him, aware that any gesture on her part would trigger an instantaneous response. Adam's arms would come alive and the urgent desire reflected on both their faces just then would be fulfilled.

The poignant moment lengthened like an orchestrated tableau—needing only one move to provide a counter one.

It was shyness which kept Toni from taking the initiative and the discovery was enough to make her pull back slightly.

As infinitesimal as her movement was, it apparently convinced Adam. Sitting up abruptly, he swung his legs over the side of the mattress and got to his feet in one lithe movement. He walked to the closet without looking back, saying as he put on his robe, "You can have the first shift in the bathroom if you like. Just don't be too long—it's later than I'd planned to get up."

He sounded almost accusing, Toni thought. As if he were blaming her for the whole embarrassing thing—which was unfair, because *she* didn't have her arms around *him*. Of course she might have been partly responsible . . .

"Look, one of us should make a move," he was saying with awful patience after he belted the robe and stepped into some leather slippers.

"You go ahead. After all, you're the one with the meeting and things to do. You won't need me for anything, will you?" Toni tried to keep her voice light and uncaring. If only he'd stop closing that closet door and come back beside her to put those strong hands to some practical use. Or if he'd say, "The hell with needing you! I want you and you want me. Why can't we go on from there?"

She wasn't allowed to linger on that daydream. Adam strode to the bathroom door, appearing profoundly relieved. "There's no reason for you to hurry. If I settle for a roll and coffee at breakfast, I'll almost be on time." He shot a look at her then as she sat on the tumbled bedclothes. "You might as well sleep in, if you want."

It was a wonder that the smoldering anger of Toni's glance didn't make the wooden bathroom door flare into flames after Adam closed it behind him.

Sleep in, indeed! Toni got out of bed just as decisively as Adam had minutes before. She marched over to the vinyl room divider and opened it. After she made sure the other end of the room was empty, she changed swiftly into her swimsuit. The sand fleas weren't supposed to work the early-morning shift and even if they did, they couldn't be as devastating as Adam Driscoll.

She pulled open the curtains to let sunshine flood into the room then and carefully averted her glance from the wide bed where she'd spent the night. But even if she closed her eyes entirely, she couldn't erase the memory of Adam beside her, with his strong, warm hands holding her so intimately.

She drew a jagged, hurting breath and let herself

out onto the porch. Not stopping for a towel or thongs, she ran swiftly for the deserted beach in front of the bungalow where the waves rolled up invitingly.

A moment later, she had plunged into the water and didn't try to contain her sobs any longer. Even if Adam came to find her on the beach before he left, there was nothing strange about a woman having wet cheeks and red eyes when she was swimming in saltwater. At least she'd used her head, Toni told herself as she turned over to float on the buoyant surface. For the first time in four days, she'd managed to do one thing right. It was just a pity that by now, it was too little and far too late.

Chapter Eight

She wasn't really surprised when Adam didn't come down to the beach at all. It was probably best that way, she decided finally, and lingered in a lounger for an extra quarter hour to be sure that she wouldn't encounter him escaping through the front door.

There was other activity around the scattered bungalows when she finally made her way back up the walk. Groups of Calabash maids with their linen carts were clustered between the units. The women avoided Toni's glance and a silence fell among them as she came within hearing. Adam wouldn't be happy at this newest sign of employee discord, she thought, forgetting her own problems for a minute. From the expression on the maids' faces, there wouldn't be much work done even before the official walkout in the afternoon.

Toni let herself back into the bungalow by the unlatched sliding door on the porch. The silence in the empty suite was almost tangible and the cool air circulated by the overhead fans made her shiver after the balmy sunshine outside.

As she walked toward the bathroom, she saw a note left prominently atop the other ice bucket on the bureau—almost as if Adam suspected that the damned receptacles drew her irresistibly to them. She gingerly picked up the piece of paper, apprehensive of its contents. A hasty scanning showed that she wasn't being sent home or told never to darken the door again. Not that his sentiments were much warmer. "Have gone on to breakfast. Will try to contact you at noon or after the meeting." That was decent of him, Toni decided on a second reading, thinking that she'd had warmer communications from her bank when she was overdrawn. "Suggest you stay on the grounds, in view of the local situation." Obviously he hadn't seen the sullen looks on the maids' faces when he'd written that. Labor disputes wouldn't improve the *joie de vivre* in any part of the resort. Adam may have had an inkling of it because he finished with, "I'll try to get your mattress changed but don't hold your breath. There's no need to worry about it, though—the way things are going there'll probably be plenty of cancellations by tonight and you can have an entire bungalow to yourself."

Perhaps he thought that possibility would cheer her as much as it undoubtedly did him. And if she'd had any sense at all, it would have. Toni told herself so as she threw his note into the wastebasket and stormed into the bathroom for her shower.

She was still muttering, "Dammit to hell!" as she toweled herself dry a little later which showed that good sense had come out a poor second to frustration. Only the discovery that she hadn't encountered any more sand fleas at the beach helped raise her spirits as she went into the other room to get dressed.

She pulled on a pair of white slacks to cover the telltale welts that still remained on her ankles and added a white scoop-neckline T-shirt. A flame-colored terry blazer went over it and she slipped on a pair of white leather loafers in case she wanted to explore the grounds of the resort afterwards.

The maids were moving slowly toward the other bungalows as Toni walked down the path leading to the dining room by the reception center. Most of the other guests were sauntering that way, too, some in cover-ups over swimsuits and a few in more formal resort fashions.

Toni was escorted to a table overlooking the ocean by a solicitous maitre d' who recommended the melon before he hurried away to seat an elderly couple. Toni managed to survey the entire dining room in the process of opening her outsized menu and confirmed what she'd suspected—Adam wasn't there.

Damn the man, she thought as she stared blindly at the bill of fare. At least he could have been civilized and lingered to share one meal with her. Even a cup of coffee and a roll could have been fun together—certainly nicer than sitting in solitary grandeur like the eighty-year-old lady at the next table. Just then, the dowager was joined by a distinguished gray-haired man and Toni sighed again.

A piece of delicious melon improved her disposition and by the time she had finished her second cup of coffee she'd resolved to stop wallowing in self-pity. The only thing necessary was to keep her dignity when dealing with Adam for the rest of their time together. It certainly shouldn't be difficult once they didn't have to share the same quarters. Toni's lips tightened a little as she thought about that. At least Adam wouldn't have any more tidbits with which to regale his friends or family after the

trip was over. As far as her own life went, there were
plenty of men at home who'd been humming around
for dates—all she had to do was take her choice. And
maybe sign up for an evening course in decorating
or tailoring—something really worthwhile. It could
be the beginning of an entirely new way of life.

"Was there something wrong with your breakfast,
madam? Something not to your liking perhaps?" It
was the maitre d' again, hovering anxiously by her
table. "I'm sorry about the service this morning.
Some of our staff called in sick."

"Everything was fine." Toni hastily managed a
more pleased expression. "I just wasn't very hun-
gry."

"You're sure, madam?"

"Quite sure." His worried expression as he looked
around at the thin platoon of waiters in the room reminded her of an old adage, "The cook was a good
cook as cooks go; and as good cooks go, she went."
Evidently the exodus had already started among
Calabash's dining-room help.

Toni left shortly afterwards, carefully skirting the
reception area where she might run into Jorge. She
hoped to see Juanito again, but she preferred a solitary encounter with the youngster. A few minutes
later, she found that he wasn't on the resort pier nor
was he aboard the Calabash launch, departing at that
moment on its morning trip to St. Thomas.

Toni stared at it broodingly, wishing that she
dared go AWOL for a shopping trip on the other island. It would be a relief to get away from all the
undercurrents at Calabash. It would also make Adam
absolutely furious if she went off again, ignoring his
orders.

She reluctantly turned away, strolling past the desk where the social director was organizing people for a tour of the Annaberg sugar mill. Once was enough for that place, Toni thought fervently, and shook her head when the hostess gave her an inquiring glance.

There must be other places to explore, Toni decided, ruling out the gift shop with its intriguing contents, to stroll across the expanse of lawn. Halfway, she was wishing that she'd brought some sort of head covering to temper the heat of the brilliant sun. Fortunately there was plenty of shade if she took the path leading up the hill behind the clay tennis courts ahead. She sauntered on, observing the people playing doubles on the nearest court with a wistful glance. They seemed to be having a wonderful time together, undeterred by the heat beating down on them.

Toni's steps quickened as she headed for the steeper and shaded part of the path. A rustle in a bush nearby made her pause until she identified a fuzzy-tailed mongoose giving her an equally leery glance. "Just make sure that you don't go down to visit your friends and relations on the beach," Toni advised him as he turned for the deeper grass. Then she started to giggle when he sat up on his back legs as if to answer back.

She climbed on up the dirt path, fascinated by the unusual flowers and the denser vegetation once she left the resort's cultivated grounds and ventured into natural growth. She stopped at one point to stare up at a termite nest in a mango tree, and later retrieved a seed pod from a mimosa to take home for a gardener friend. The trees thinned farther along, giving a bird's-eye view of the gorgeous resort acres below, and she sat down to rest on a fallen tree trunk, while enjoying the scene.

When she reached the summit, she found that the section of path going down the other side was really too steep for comfort. No wonder she hadn't met any hikers coming the other way! Either she had to retrace her footsteps or find an easier way to return. Then she caught a glimpse of aqua water through the trees at the other side of the resort and realized that she would descend to Dolphin Cove. It was a beach section of Calabash renowned for its beauty, so she decided to go on.

To keep her mind from the sharp drop at the edge of the path to the right, she hummed a jingle about "eating peas with honey." She rendered it absently as she tried to avoid slipping on the loose grit of the path's surface during her cautious descent. When she passed the worst part, she changed to a clear contralto, finishing with, "They do taste kind of funny but it keeps them on my knife." Before she could go into a second chorus, a commotion on the beach below made her forget all about music.

She stopped to stare down at the familiar figures on a patio beside one of Calabash's more luxurious bungalows. Jorge Benitez was deep in conversation with the bearded man who was his brother's aide. The same man who just the day before had been in the pickup truck at the Annaberg Ruins and a day or so before that had been patronizing a voodoo shop in New Orleans. Toni knew in her bones that he'd been busy carrying out Rafael Benitez' orders both times and that the general strike scheduled at Calabash that afternoon was part of their overall plan. From the looks of things, Jorge was another willing accomplice to the goings-on.

A shout of childish laughter drew her glance to the beach in front of the bungalow where Juanito, in shorts and shirt, had suddenly discovered one of the tiny rabbits on the island huddled beneath a palm tree. His nursemaid who was knitting in a lounge chair near the patio steps looked up to utter some command which the youngster promptly ignored. His father and the bearded man stopped talking just long enough to see what was happening and then went back to their noisy discussion.

Toni felt a premonition of dread as her glance returned to Juanito who was inexpertly stalking the rabbit in the role of mighty hunter. The nursemaid gave him an exasperated glance before going on with her knitting.

Only the rabbit was taking Juanito seriously and decided to try for better cover. Abandoning the palm tree, he neatly cut around the corner of the bungalow at the last second, choosing the hard-surfaced path up the hillside rather than disappearing into the underbrush. With a gleeful cry, Juanito came after it.

Toni was still a hundred feet up at the last switchback as she watched the chase coming her way. She smiled at the small boy's futile efforts to catch the little brown animal and would have stayed an amused spectator if she hadn't suddenly heard his father's stricken shout of "Juanito! *Ven aquí!* Juanito!"

There was anguish in that last word. Toni was conscious of Jorge leaping off the patio in pursuit of the boy even as her frantic glance scoured the dirt track to determine why.

One look was enough and, forgetting all about loose grit and the danger of falling, Toni tore down the last part of the path shrieking, "Juanito—don't!"

The shock of a strange voice and figure flying down at him made the youngster pull up, bewildered, just inches from the red-painted branch of a manchineel tree. The rabbit whisked around the trunk of the tree and disappeared into the thick grass beyond.

Before Juanito could follow his quarry, Toni swooped down beside him and caught his shoulders in a firm grip. "I'm sorry, sweetie, you can't go in there," she said breathlessly. He'd just started to whimper at such strange happenings, when his father pounded up the path and swung the boy into his arms. On the beach, the nursemaid watched wide-eyed, her knitting forgotten at her feet.

Jorge murmured something comforting in Spanish as Juanito buried his face in his father's shoulder. When the little boy's sobs started to subside, the Calabash manager stared accusingly at Toni's quiet figure beside him.

"You are the last person I expected to see here!" His tone was ragged and his accent more noticeable than it had been the day before.

"I was just walking." Toni gestured at the path as if to make up for her inadequate comment. She was still trembling from Juanito's close call but she swallowed over the lump in her throat to say, "I don't know about the zoning laws in St. John but frankly I'd either put an axe to that thing"—she jerked her head toward the manchineel tree—"or build a high fence."

"Believe me, I feel the same way." A flickering

muscle in the manager's cheek showed how tensely he was holding his jaw. "I haven't spent much time at this part of Calabash. Otherwise I certainly would not have let Juanito run free." His arms tightened around the boy who was still nuzzling in his shoulder.

There was no doubting the sincerity of Jorge's words and Toni smiled sympathetically in response as she prepared to go on down the path. "It's all right for me to walk here, isn't it? I didn't realize that the trail came out practically in your back yard."

"That's not my bungalow." Jorge lowered his son to the walk but kept a tight grip on the youngster's hand as he motioned Toni ahead of them. "It belongs to an acquaintance of mine."

"The man you were talking to? He seems to have disappeared."

Jorge pushed Juanito ahead of him and bit off a terse command in Spanish. It must have told the boy to go on down to his waiting nursemaid because the youngster's lip quivered and for a moment he looked rebellious, but after seeing the expression on his father's face he obediently scurried back toward the beach. "Now, then"—Jorge put out a hand to keep Toni beside him—"exactly what do you know about that man?"

"Not much." And that was certainly telling the truth, she thought. "He looks familiar. Didn't we see him at the sugar-mill ruins yesterday?"

Juanito provided an unexpected diversion at that point. Apparently he was taking out his rebellion on his nursemaid and she'd countered with a sharp slap on his bottom. As he let out a howl of protest, his father groaned. "*Dios!* More trouble. That child has been crying most of the time since he arrived. I must go down and sort things out."

"Of course. Probably he misses his mother. It's a pity that the three of you can't be here together."

"I told you—"

"Oh, I know." She smiled briefly back at him as she started on down the path again. "But time has a way of solving lots of problems. Maybe your wife is feeling differently about things now, too. I'd guess that she's missing Juanito—and you—very much."

"Miss Morgan! Toni—wait please."

The command uttered in Jorge's deep voice was impossible to ignore and Toni lingered reluctantly by the corner of the patio when she reached level ground.

"I'm deeply in your debt," Jorge said as he caught up with her. "After what happened yesterday—what I did and what I said to you—" He broke off to rub his forehead tiredly. "I don't even know where to start with my apologies."

"Oh, please—just forget it."

"And the fact that you saved my son from harm. Should I forget that, too?"

"You'd have done the same thing. Anybody would." Toni kept her voice light. "I'm just glad that I was on the spot. You *can* do me a favor though."

Jorge shot a quick glance at the curtained windows of the bungalow even as he said soberly, "If it is in my power—anything."

Toni bit down on the soft inner edge of her lip as she thought about that. Maybe the smart thing would be to ask what devilment Rafael and his friend had planned. Certainly Adam and his clients needed any help they could get. Then she realized that Jorge Benitez' code of behavior didn't allow for feminine interference in business affairs. He wasn't about to stage a confessional and betray his brother out of gratitude for a trifling incident. She took a deep, unsteady breath and went back to her original question. "It may sound silly but I've lost my bearings. Could you point me in the right direction to get back to my bungalow? This weather's too warm for any wrong turns."

Jorge's forehead smoothed as if by magic. "Of course. I can even do better than that," he said as a station wagon with the Calabash insignia turned into the drive and the driver got out to deliver a package. "I'll take that, Lonzo," the manager told him. "Would you give Miss Morgan here a ride back to the reception center?"

A wide smile split the man's face and Toni realized it was the first evidence of enthusiasm she'd seen from an employee since she'd arrived. "Yessir, Mr. Benitez. Right away."

"Thank you very much." Toni's grateful smile encompassed both men and she walked over to get in the passenger seat.

Jorge was right behind her to close the station-wagon door, after taking time to deposit the package on the corner of the patio. "I shall look forward to seeing you soon, Toni. Perhaps sooner than you think."

She didn't have time to ask him what he meant by that. Even as her lips formed the question, the driver put the station wagon in reverse, using a heavy foot on the accelerator that had the wheels spinning on the loose gravel of the road. An instant later, he shifted into "drive," even before they'd stopped going backwards. He made short work of the side road from the Dolphin Cove bungalows, reaching the main circle drive of Calabash a few minutes later where he pulled to a stop, gunning the engine impatiently.

"Do you have to go straight back to the reception center, ma'am," he said, "or do you have time to detour by the Hogshead Bay section with me? It's only a few miles down here to the right and the housekeeper needs the extra linen I've got in the back."

"Hogshead Bay will be fine. It seems good to sit and ride after walking in the sun all morning." Toni didn't add that she really wasn't in any hurry to get back to the empty rooms of the cottage and try to fill time for the rest of the day.

The driver seemed relieved by her answer. He made an effort after that to point out the local items of interest, like the restored stone fences of brain coral and brick which were patterned after ones built during Danish rule on the island. Later additions included handmade yellowish brick and ballast stones, brought in by freight boats when the sugar plantations were in their heyday. The driver was so intent on pointing out the historical remnants that he almost missed the turnoff to Hogshead Bay later on and had to swing wide for the circular entrance. Toni noted that this section of Calabash resembled a rambling old manor house complete with outbuildings. They were all perched high on a gentle hillside which provided a fabulous view of the greenish-blue waters beneath. Apparently all sections of the resort had been designed to fit the topographical contours of the land and, although distinct in style, were equally charming. It was no wonder that Adam's clients were chewing their corporate nails over what was going to happen in the future, Toni thought.

The driver made his linen delivery in remarkably short time and apologized for keeping Toni waiting when he returned.

"I didn't mind a bit," she told him truthfully. "I was sure that our place on the beach was the prettiest I'd seen until I discovered Dolphin Cove this morning. Now, after viewing this"—she gestured toward the gray fieldstone and weathered wood of the manor house—"I'd like to spend a month at Hogshead Bay. I suppose that name came from the old days, too."

"Yes, ma'am. The name's about all that's left. Oh, there are a few sections restored by the Park Service where the original owners built of bulletwood but termites took care of the rest of the buildings. Usually there's just a big royal palm left or maybe a tamarind at the old places. Vines come along and cover the rest of the ruins. You have to be strong to survive on St. John." The last sentence was said almost under his breath.

Toni thought of the manchineel trees scattered over the island and nodded. Thank heaven, Juanito hadn't run headfirst into disaster at the very beginning of his holiday. Although maybe the near-tragedy would have unexpected side benefits. His father might reconsider his marital woes and see that the little boy needed both parents watching over him instead of sporadic visits to satisfy terms of the legal separation.

Toni was so engrossed in her thoughts that she was unaware of how quickly the miles were slipping by and they'd pulled up at the bus stop behind the reception center before she realized it.

She thanked the driver and cut across the green lawn to the path leading to the bungalow, sternly denying her inclination to detour by the Tower restaurant where guests could be seen enjoying midday cocktails. They looked supremely content as they lounged by the stone barricade, and surveyed the lush tropical grounds beneath them. Toni wondered if they'd be as content in a few hours when resort activity was scheduled to grind to a halt. She smiled wryly and decided that ignorance could be a blessing after all.

She'd certainly be happier if she hadn't known that Adam would still be missing when she got to their bungalow just ahead of her. It looked more appealing than ever with its frame of palms and the towering turpentine or gumbo limbo trees just beyond. Toni wondered dismally whether she or Adam would be the one to move later in the day. He'd probably decide that the manor house at Hogshead Bay would be the place for her. That way, there'd be plenty of space between them during their remaining time on the island.

She unlocked the bungalow door and went inside, walking over to put her clutch purse on the bureau and check the nearby ice bucket. It was filled to the brim with a new delivery. Her lips tightened as she replaced the lid and walked on past the vinyl curtain to discover that someone had removed her damp mattress and box spring, leaving only four indentations in the rug to show for it. Adam hadn't wasted any time, she thought dispiritedly, and then noticed the second ice bucket still on her end table. Peering inside, she saw it was full to the brim with fresh cubes, too.

"Great!" she muttered. "I can throw them at the next mouse that walks past. Damn it all! What a way to spend a vacation."

She pulled off her clothes and tossed them onto her open suitcase, hoping that a cool shower would help her appearance and possibly improve her flagging spirits.

She lingered under the tepid water until her fingers took on a prunelike appearance and then got out to towel herself vigorously. It was necessary to steal one of Adam's clean towels to dry her hair after she donned a thigh-length terry robe but she only hesitated a moment before plucking it from the rack. At least it would give them something to argue about when he came back. The same perverse quirk made her leave the mat in the middle of the room and her damp towel tossed over the shower bar. Probably she'd weaken and tidy things later, but at the moment even brief defiance helped her wounded pride.

She was still toweling her damp hair as she went into the bedroom again, nearly collapsing when a strange masculine voice said, "Too bad you had to spoil things by coming out. I was looking forward to meeting you in the shower."

Toni whipped the towel off and gasped as she saw Rafael's bearded henchman standing on the other side of the room by Adam's open suitcase. "My God, what are you doing here?"

"Just what it looks like, lady." He flicked disdainfully through a pile of clean shirts in the suitcase and then, deliberately, shoved the bag off the luggage rack, spewing the contents onto the floor in an unholy mess. "You've had it easy up till now but the boss is tired of you poking your nose in his business." He smoothed the beard at his jawline which was apparently his only concession to vanity. He was wearing the same plaid shirt and rumpled cotton pants he'd had on when he was with Jorge on the patio earlier that morning. If her memory wasn't at fault, he'd worn the same outfit at the sugar mill the day before. The man was at least fifty pounds overweight and the heat and humidity obviously bothered him more than most people. At that moment, he looked like a surly bull. He sounded like one, too, as he said, "You shouldn't have let the boyfriend drag you into this."

"Mr. Driscoll isn't my boyfriend. I'm just working for him," Toni said, determined to set the record straight.

"Sure you are." His thick lips curved unpleasantly. "Not exactly the usual kind of nine-to-five, but you can't complain about the fringe benefits. I get them on my job, too." There was an instant's pause. "You're going to be one of them."

"That's ridiculous," Toni snapped, trying the hide the qualms his words gave her. "You can't tell me that Rafael Benitez would sanction anything like that here at Calabash. It sounds like an old Capone movie."

He walked over to pull the drapes closed on the porch with an economy of movement surprising in one of his weight. "Didn't I tell you? Chicago's my home town. The touch comes naturally to me. Especially when I'm around a br—" He broke off and substituted, ". . . a lady like you. I don't know why you're blowing your stack. Driscoll's not apt to be around for a while—the Benitez boys have taken care of that. Behave yourself and you'll be money ahead. Otherwise—" He moistened his heavy lips and started toward her.

Toni took an instinctive step backward, wondering whether to make a dash for the outside door behind her or try for the bathroom and lock herself in.

"Don't get any bright ideas, lady." He must have known the way her thoughts were going because he moved to cut off any retreat. "You wouldn't get far and you *would* get hurt. I can promise you that."

"Put one finger on me and I'll scream the roof off. And you're wrong about not being interrupted. Adam might not come but Jorge will," she threatened, trying a wild chance.

The man's thick eyebrows flew up before descending to a threatening line. "That's a crock if I ever heard one. He doesn't have time for fun and games any more than Driscoll. They're all in that meeting down at the main office."

"That wasn't what he told me on the path after you disappeared," she said, elated by her apparent success. "You're not the only one who didn't plan on being interrupted."

"He didn't say anything to me about it."

"Why should he? You're just Rafael's hired hand. Good for stealing luggage and breaking into bungalows." She stalled for time. "Did you honestly think I wouldn't connect you with that awful voodoo doll? After seeing you behind me in the Quarter that morning in New Orleans?"

"Putting it in your bag was Rafael's idea." He

thrust his head forward and looked more like an angry bull than ever. "We didn't give a damn what you suspected. If it had been up to me, I'd have left a bomb in the suitcase. That way, we could have taken care of both of you in Puerto Rico. Maybe next time the boss'll listen."

"I don't care about next time." Toni managed another step backward and felt behind her for the knob to the outside door. "You'd better get out of here now if you want to go in one piece. If Jorge finds you here, he'll think—"

"—that I'm just following orders. Once I tell him that Rafael has other plans for you—" The man broke off as he saw her turn to struggle with the door. "Leave that alone, you little—"

What he would have called her never was known because as her fingers yanked frantically on the knob, the door was pushed open, smashing into her at the same instant the bearded man clutched her shoulder.

"Let me *go!*" Toni shouted, shoving at his massive chest. She twisted and saw the man on the threshold. "Adam! Thank God!"

"Get your hands off her, you bastard!" Adam yanked her aside in a single violent motion, his other fist coming up to connect with that bearded jaw.

The savage uppercut hit the man when he was already off balance. He fell sideways onto the floor with a thud which shook the furniture and made the lamp sway.

He lay there stunned for a moment and then pushed up to a sitting position, shaking his head. "You lousy creep—" he started in a vicious undertone only to have Adam cut him off.

"Stow it and get the hell out of here." Adam only

took his attention from the man long enough to put some keys into Toni's hand and shove her urgently across the threshold. "My car's out there. Get in and drive to the reception center."

"But Adam—"

"Don't argue, dammit! Get going!" he snapped, turning to face the other man who was lurching painfully erect.

"I can't leave you here with him!" Toni wailed.

"You little fool! Do as I tell you!"

"Let her stick around to watch," the heavy-set man sneered as he flexed his fingers. "I have plans for her afterwards—just the two of us. After I mop the floor with you, lover-boy."

"That's enough, Curt!" The order came from the man who had just slid aside the glass door and stepped into the room. "You have exceeded your duties once too often," Jorge Benitez said in a biting undertone that sliced through the air like cold steel. "My brother will not be pleased. Especially now— when he's changed his mind."

The bearded man swung to face him, keeping his hamlike fists clenched. "What the hell are you talking about?"

"Don't use that tone with me! Or have you forgotten who gives the final orders?" The manager's aristocratic features were even more aloof than usual as he stared back at the heavy-set man.

"Rafael's the one who told me to come—"

"My brother has changed his mind. Don't make me repeat it again." There was something infinitely more ominous about the measured undertone than the other's blustering protest.

Adam had been listening to the exchange with

narrowed eyes. "Maybe you'd be kind enough to let us know the new set of orders," he said derisively after Jorge's pronouncement.

"I can understand your impatience, Mr. Driscoll." The manager's expressionless tone showed his reluctance to indulge in explanation. "Bear with me a little longer."

"Do I have a choice?"

Jorge couldn't fail to notice his sarcasm and a wave of red crept under the olive skin at his cheekbones. "I know the present situation isn't to your liking . . ."

"That's an understatement," Adam interrupted, rubbing his knuckles.

". . . but I promise that your associates will be gratified," Jorge persisted.

Adam wasn't impressed. "If you think I'm going to stand around after I found this ghoul threatening Miss Morgan, you're out of your mind. I don't care what Rafael has decided from here on. There's a charge of breaking and entering plus assault to deal with first."

The man called Curt scowled and took a threatening step toward Adam, but Jorge spat out a Spanish word that stopped the bearded one in his tracks.

"Get out of here, Curt," Jorge went on. "My brother is at the bungalow and after that, you both have a plane to catch."

Curt's thick lips were compressed with anger but he stomped past Benitez out onto the porch facing the beach. An instant later, the sound of his heavy footsteps dimmed and finally disappeared altogether.

Adam moved to face Jorge angrily. "There's

plenty of time for us to swear out a complaint before that plane can leave Cruz Bay."

"Exactly. And if you still feel the same way after I tell you what is going to happen here at Calabash—" Benitez shrugged elegant shoulders and walked over to lounge against one of the upholstered chairs. Then he noticed that Toni was still watching the scene with wide eyes, the towel which she'd been using to dry her hair hanging from her nerveless grasp at her side. "I'm sorry, *querida*," Jorge said, getting hastily to his feet again.

"Oh, for heaven's sake, sit down," she told him. "I'll just go in and . . ."

"Get some clothes on," Adam finished for her, as his stern gaze took in the brevity of her terry robe. Toni hastily tightened the belt and smoothed the lapels into place.

"If Toni isn't too uncomfortable, I'd like her to hear this," Jorge said before she could follow Adam's dictate.

"I'm fine," she assured him, keeping her glance averted from Adam's suddenly stony one. "Besides, I won't catch cold in this climate and if I turn off the overhead fan there isn't even a draft." Reaching over to the wall switch, she flipped it and watched the brass blades slow to a stop. "There—now I'm all set," she said and settled onto a nearby rattan chest.

"Oh, hell!" Adam said half under his breath. He gestured for Jorge to sit down but prowled restlessly around the room himself. "This will have to be a fast recital. I was due at that meeting fifteen minutes ago."

"I know. I wasted time looking for you there. That's why I was late following up on Curt."

Adam's jaw tightened as he stared across the room at the Calabash manager. "You mean that you knew you'd find him here? My God, you've got a nerve to sit there and admit it."

"I didn't send him, Mr. Driscoll. My brother only told me about the man after we'd settled a few things." He raised a hand when Adam would have interrupted again. "Let me finish, please. I wanted to inform you that there will be no slowdown—no strike today. Nor in the future. Your associates at the meeting should be pleased to hear it."

Adam looked completely dumbfounded at the other's announcement. His piercing glance lingered on Jorge's satisfied countenance for a considerable time and then swung to Toni who wasn't bothering to hide her elation. "All right, I'll bite," Adam said finally. "What's the gimmick? It's too late for New Year's resolutions and too early for Christmas donations."

"You're suspicious, Mr. Driscoll?"

"There's a lot of money involved, Mr. Benitez." Adam faithfully mocked the other's tone. "Your brother isn't noted for philanthropy and he's cost us plenty already. Bankers weren't happy about lending money when Rafael was threatening to destroy the new construction here and planning a political take-over on the island."

"I know what my brother has done in the past— you don't have to remind me. I was not altogether unsympathetic at the time. But now, I've changed my mind."

"And that automatically changes your brother's? I'll need more proof before presenting the meeting with that."

"You won't get a signed confession, if that's what you mean." Jorge stood up, his face bleak. "I give you my word as head of the Benitez family that Rafael won't interfere with the affairs of Calabash today or in the future. He's also promised to refrain from any personal involvement in the politics here on St. John. Is that satisfactory?"

"Adam, don't be so stiff-necked," Toni pleaded, unable to keep quiet any longer. "Can't you see Jorge means it? I don't know how he worked the miracle but it's wonderful!"

The manager's expression softened at her enthusiasm. "I didn't think you'd need any explanations, my dear Toni. Actually, you brought the whole thing about."

"With Rafael?" Adam's face was a cold mask by then.

"Certainly not," Jorge said. "As the elder son, I am the head of our family and control all the finances. It's as simple as that."

"Then maybe you'd tell me what the hell Toni has to do with this decision?"

"I'd be delighted to," Jorge said, smiling for the first time. "Especially since I'm sure you won't hear anything about what happened this morning from her."

Toni decided to stop the embarrassing confessional right then and there. "I thought you had to get to your meeting," she said to Adam. "Jorge can tell you about it another time if it's really necessary."

"As a matter of fact, I can tell you on the way," the manager said, looking at his watch. "I should be down there, too. The chef had special instructions for refreshments afterward and I don't want anything to go wrong."

Jorge had the brisk assured air of a man who'd settled all of his pressing problems but Adam looked as if he'd lost the skirmish instead of coming out on the winning side. He walked reluctantly to the door with the other saying, "So I'm just supposed to forget all about pressing criminal charges?"

Jorge pulled up to shrug, Latin-fashion. "As you said before, it's early for Christmas giving but if you could be generous with Curt and Rafael's part in all this, Calabash would avoid unpleasant publicity."

"Hell! I suppose you're right." Adam reached for the doorknob but hesitated before turning it, as he stared over his shoulder at Toni. "If you're not here when I get back this time, I hope you'll leave a note. It's too important to risk any more misunderstandings."

He opened the door then and almost walked into a maid who was standing, key in hand, on the front porch. There was a florist's box under her other arm, along with a stack of clean linen. Adam jerked his head for her to go on in, while he waited for Jorge to join him. He didn't hide his disapproval as he watched the manager press Toni's fingers between his palms and say, "Juanito and I will be pleased to see you later. It's important for you to meet a special member of the family who's flying in from Puerto Rico this afternoon."

"Jorge—that's wonderful!" Toni tried to ignore Adam's disturbing scrutiny from the sidelines. "We can get together somehow. Give my love to Juanito in the meantime."

"I'll do that. He's a different boy already. You

were right this morning . . ." He let his voice drop as Adam cleared his throat. "Never mind, we'll talk later."

Before following him down the porch steps, Adam bestowed a bleak look which encompassed both Toni and the maid who had put her belongings down, obviously waiting for people to get out of her way so she could get to work. As if recognizing the futility of saying any more, his lips tightened and he went out, slamming the door behind him.

Chapter Nine

Toni stared at that closed door as she stood quietly by the rattan chest. When it was obvious that she wasn't going to move, the maid shrugged resignedly and asked, "You want me to fix the flowers, ma'am?"

"What? Oh, the flowers." Toni directed a vague glance toward the box that the woman had put on the bureau. "I guess so. If you don't mind." Even as she made the conventional comment, her thoughts were recalling the unhappy look on Adam's proud countenance as he'd gone out the door. If it had been anyone else, she would have thought that "discouraged" was the adjective that applied. Which was ridiculous, she decided, going back into the bathroom to find a comb for her nearly dry hair. Probably he was just angry at having to let that man Curt get off scot-free. Toni closed her eyes for an instant and shuddered, thinking what might have happened to her.

If Adam had been dressed in shining armor, he couldn't have been more impressive when he'd arrived at that crucial time. It was just her luck to be looking like a rumpled bedspread when everything happened, she thought, surveying her reflection in the mirror. No wonder that Adam turned her down.

The terrible pun surfaced slowly in her consciousness and she groaned aloud. Lord! She was in worse shape than she thought.

"Is there anything wrong, ma'am?" The maid came to the threshold, viewing her with concern.

"No, I was just thinking of something." Toni's eyes widened as she saw the magnificent rose bouquet the woman held. "Those are beautiful in that cutglass vase!" She leaned forward to sniff one of the barely open scarlet buds. "Umm. Calabash certainly treats guests royally."

The woman looked as if she were going to contradict her and then shrugged again. "You want to read the card?" she asked.

Toni shook her head. "No, thanks. I can guess what it says. 'Compliments of the management' or 'Best wishes for a pleasant stay.' Just put it on the bureau so Mr. Driscoll will see it when he comes back. If you want some water for that vase, I'm finished in here."

"I can come back later if you'd rather, ma'am. I just have to change the beds and the towels."

"You can do it now. I'm going into the other room and get dressed." She lingered to ask, "Do you know when they're going to put the other bed back in?"

"No, ma'am. I 'spect it'll take a while. Mattresses come from the warehouse at Cruz Bay. There's no hurry, is there? You've still got two beds." More than enough for two people. The last was left unsaid, but there was no doubt as to her meaning.

Color flared in Toni's cheeks under the woman's speculative gaze. "Yes. Yes, of course. I just wondered." She managed a polite smile which didn't have any more meaning than her words and escaped around the vinyl partition. It was ridiculous to have asked the question in the first place. How could the maid be expected to be bursting with information? Especially when Adam hadn't given a rush order to replace that miserable mattress.

Toni tossed aside her robe but her fingers became motionless on the clasp of the bra she was fastening as another thought occurred to her. Since the employees' strike had been called off, wasn't it reasonable to suppose that the Calabash guests would stay put? Certainly there was no reason for them to strike off like a bunch of lemmings to St. Thomas when they could soak up sunshine where they were. Which meant that there wouldn't be any extra beds or bungalows as Adam had forecast.

Toni chewed uncertainly on the edge of her lip and went on dressing slowly, wondering what she could do about it. Adam hadn't hidden his dislike of their status quo but he certainly wouldn't approve of any magnanimous gestures on her part for the coming night. Not that she was even tempted to make them. The sand fleas might restrict their activities to the beach when darkness came but the mosquitos felt no such compulsion. A night on the porch would be sheer horror even if she could manage to drag a lounge there.

That left two alternatives, Toni decided. She could wait and see what Adam suggested or she could pack and be ready to board the evening launch to St. Thomas. There were plenty of hotels there and she could always use the attraction of duty-free shopping as her excuse. The more she thought about the latter idea—the better it seemed.

She pulled on the skirt of her bone-colored silk suit after donning a matching blouse with a slash neckline. Beige leather espadrilles would be suitable either in St. Thomas or Calabash, she told herself, and then bestowed a mental jab for trying to cling to an obviously lost cause.

Adam didn't need her around any longer. The fact was as obvious as the sand-flea bites on her ankle that she was absently scratching just then. That meant St. Thomas—and establishing a safe distance between them.

Toni was roused from her decision by the maid poking her head around the vinyl partition. "I'm finished now, ma'am. The man'll be in with some more ice a little later—unless you want it right away."

"No, thanks. I've had enough for a lifetime."

"Ma'am?"

A sheepish expression washed over Toni's face. "Sorry. I was thinking of something else. There's no hurry for the ice. I'll just be packing."

"You checking out?" The woman consulted a slip of paper from the pocket of her uniform. "It don't say nothing 'bout it here."

"I just made up my mind." Toni confessed, wishing that she had kept quiet. "Actually nothing's settled."

The maid pursed her lips disapprovingly. "You'll have to let them know at reception. There's a long waiting list here at Calabash. Maybe I'd better tell the housekeeper."

"Heavens, no! Besides, Mr. Driscoll will be here. I'm the only one who'll be leaving."

Disapproval changed to tolerant amusement. "Does your man know?"

"He's not my—" Toni stopped abruptly and started over. "I think it would be better"—she hesitated again, searching for the right words—"better to forget the whole thing," she concluded lamely.

"Yes, ma'am. I think so, too. That's why folks come to Calabash—to forget 'bout being unhappy." The older woman gathered her belongings. "I left that bouquet on the bureau and the card right beside it. You can't miss seeing it."

Toni shook her head wryly after she'd gone and turned back to her packing. If she didn't watch out, the maid would be bringing a love amulet with the next change of bed linen. "It's probably all your fault," she informed the voodoo doll as she ran across it in a layer of tissue. "I should have consigned you to the round file long ago." She looked at a wastebasket nearby and hefted the doll in her palm, trying to make up her mind. It was ridiculous to keep the thing, she told herself—even as she rewrapped it and started to put it in her suitcase. That showed how far gone she was! Keeping a horror like that just because it was all she had to remember the trip and being with Adam.

Her figure stayed motionless for an instant and then she tossed the doll into the wastebasket with a decisive gesture. From now on, she'd concentrate on the future.

She was so intent on closing her suitcase that she missed the sound of the glass door opening behind her. The first inkling she had that she wasn't alone was when Adam's voice said, "So you've decided to leave." It was a statement rather than a question and, from the way he lounged against the edge of the door, he might have been announcing rain before sunset. "Should I be flattered that you stuck around long enough to say good-bye?" he continued, "Or were you just going to leave a note?"

Toni ignored that, saying breathlessly, "You scared me out of five years' growth. Doesn't anybody ever knock in this place?"

His eyebrows climbed. "I live here. Why in the hell should I knock?"

"Because—because, oh, for heaven's sake—you know what I mean. You could have coughed or called out, or something. Anything except creeping up on a person."

"I did not creep up."

"Well, sidle in the door, then."

"And I didn't sidle anywhere, dammit!"

"You don't have to shout."

"Then get it straight. I didn't creep, sidle, ooze, or crawl into this room. I walked in like any normal human being. And what happens? I get my head taken off." He shoved his hands into his pockets and pushed himself away from the door. "Nora acts the same way when she has a guilty conscience."

Because he was entirely too astute in his reasoning, Toni employed another tack to divert him. "My conscience has nothing to do with it. Curt came in through that same door and I'm trying not to remember."

Adam had the decency to show momentary chagrin at hearing that but he rallied quickly. "Well, you can forget that gorilla—your chum has promised that he'll be off the island within the hour."

"You should furnish a program so I'll know who you're talking about," she said, showing that Adam couldn't corner the market on sarcasm. "Exactly which chum do you mean?"

"Oh, for God's sake, Toni. Isn't it a little late for playing games?" Adam remarked, prowling the room.

Normally his unhappy appeal would have left her putty in his hands but Toni was still smarting over his abrupt withdrawal from her side that morning. There hadn't been any sympathy or understanding of her feelings then. All he'd thought about was putting paid to an embarrassing bedtime experience, ignoring her reaction entirely. He'd provided an education in doing it—but it was in frustration rather than fulfillment and if she stayed around asking for more of the same, she really was a case.

Toni's resolution stiffened even more as he suddenly retrieved the voodoo doll from the wastebasket and said accusingly, "I'll be damned! You really couldn't wait to toss out everything, could you? I'm surprised that you didn't get rid of the roses, too."

Toni didn't see what a bunch of flowers provided by the Calabash management had to do with their discussion, except that at that moment, she suspected Adam would have quarreled with St. Peter about gate passes.

"You're being absurd." She snatched the doll from him and propped it against the mirror of the dressing table just for something to do. "I didn't want to keep it because of Curt—every time I looked at it, I'd see those horrible fat fingers of his pushing it into my suitcase. But I can keep it around if you insist. I should warn you, though," she added aloofly, "if you feel a sudden pain, a doctor won't help."

Adam sank onto the arm of one of the upholstered chairs and shrugged. "I expected it before now."

"I don't see why." Her tone softened involuntarily. "You have me completely confused. You're not supposed to even be here. What about that meeting?"

"Jorge was telling the directors all they wanted to know. There was no reason for me to hang around—especially when I thought there were more important things to do. Incidentally, he told me what you did on the path for Juanito this morning. I can see why he's grateful."

Adam's tone was reverting to normal but his expression was still hard to fathom. It made Toni think of the maps from the Middle Ages with their blank unexplored spots. Or the Elizabethan charts which marked the unknown with "wilderness" or "Here be dragons." The dragons fitted Adam better, she decided. Certainly he had some sort of beast haunting him just then.

"As a matter of fact," he was continuing in the same bleak voice, "Jorge is a pretty decent guy. I can understand why you'd like him."

"I hardly know him but now that he has his priorities sorted out—he should be much happier."

"That's what he said." Adam was staring moodily at the toe of his shoe. "Something about the mistake he'd made—underestimating the power of a woman. Although I'm damned if I can see any future for you in it." He frowned as he looked up to meet her gaze. "Latin families don't condone divorce, even these days. His wife and son will win out no matter what he's intimated to you."

Toni's heart did a double flip. "Well, I should hope so. I don't know what he told you on the way to that meeting but his wife is arriving this afternoon for a reconciliation attempt. I'd put next month's salary on its success. Juanito had this one wired all along."

"Then where do you come in? I thought you were meeting Jorge later."

"He wants to introduce me to his wife, that's all. There was never anything between us otherwise. He was all mixed up and I just came along at the right time. Why, I hardly know the man."

"Yet you're all packed and ready to go." Adam gestured to her closed suitcases. "If it's not for Benitez' benefit, what's the hurry?"

His last comment made her temper flare again. "You mean that you actually thought I was going to play musical bungalows from here on? Well, thanks very much—it's nice to know what kind of a reputation you've given me."

"Don't change the subject," he snapped back. "I want to know why you're packed."

"Because I was going shopping in St. Thomas," Toni said, not quite daring to confess that she'd planned to spend the rest of her time there, as well. "You said you weren't sure about what accommodations we'd have for the rest of our stay so I thought I'd be ready to move."

"That's an understatement. You were practically running down the front steps. So much for my powers of persuasion."

"They weren't great," she acknowledged, determined not to let him know how much his indifference had hurt. She picked up one suitcase and moved it purposefully into the other part of the room near the front door. When she saw that Adam had trailed her but hadn't bothered to bring her other case, she continued bitterly, "That note of yours wasn't the kind you wrap in blue ribbon."

"Maybe not, but I never thought you'd take it this way." The color had left his face and suddenly he sounded like a man who had been goaded too far as he started toward the door. "I'm going down to the reception center and find another room even if I have to move your friend Jorge and sleep on his desk. Do me a favor and get rid of those stinking flowers before I come back."

His vehemence brought her head up. "What do you mean?"

He stopped, his hand on the door. "Just exactly what I said. And when you're tossing them out, dump my note into the wastebasket with them." He gestured toward the small envelope the maid had left propped against the vase of roses. "Since it was so damned offensive, I'm surprised you didn't tear it up before now." He turned and would have yanked the door open except that Toni had put on the chain so he had to fumble to remove it.

"Adam, wait!" Toni flew to his side, pulling his hand from the knob. "Please—" Her fingers went up to cover his mouth when he started to object. "Just listen a minute. I was talking about the note where you told me not to hope for a mattress. Was there another one?"

"You mean you didn't even see *that* one?" He

jerked his chin in the direction of the bureau but kept his gaze locked on hers.

Her palms went up to her cheeks in horror as she realized what she'd done. "I thought it came from the management. Like the flowers. You mean that *you* sent them. To me?" Color flooded her pale face. "Oh, Adam! How could I have been such a fool? I'll read it right now."

His hand caught her before she could move more than a half step away. "No, you don't."

She stared up at him in bewilderment. "Why not?"

"Because I can tell you what's in it." His grip tightened and he pulled her back in front of him. "And I don't intend to let you get that far from me ever again if I can help it."

Toni's eyes widened in amazement and delight. This new Adam, gazing so earnestly down at her, was a far cry from the man who had stomped out the door less than an hour before. She wanted to pinch herself to see if she was dreaming but it wasn't worth the effort. Not after spending the entire trip maneuvering to get close! "I thought you couldn't wait to attend that meeting so you could make arrangements for the rest of our stay," she accused.

"I couldn't wait to get out of here because I thought you intended to spend the rest of your time at Calabash with Jorge Benitez," he corrected.

"Adam! You weren't jealous?"

"I never have been before," he said almost wonderingly, "but when he was standing here kissing your hand, I almost punched him in the jaw—just like his friend Curt."

"I didn't dream you felt like that. You were so

cold and forbidding, I thought you couldn't stand the sight of me. Why didn't you say something before?" Toni managed to get a hand free so she could gently touch his cheek and then drew in her breath sharply when he turned his head and bestowed a soft kiss in her palm.

He grinned at her breathless response. "What do you think I was doing in New Orleans at that breakfast table?" When she looked perplexed, he said, "My darling goose, I didn't need a companion for the trip but I *did* need a good excuse to get you under my roof for a while so we could know each other better. Rafael provided it." His slow grin appeared. "I didn't dream that *you'd* provide an excuse for sharing my bed."

"I knew you didn't believe me last night! Fine thing!" She tried to sound indignant.

"Fine thing indeed! That was my reaction, too, when you first got in beside me. Especially since I had fallen completely in love with you long before then. But after an entire night of trying to keep my distance—when every instinct was telling me just the opposite—I gave up."

Her glance met his, measuringly. "Did you? I had the feeling this morning that you were leaving it up to me."

"You're right about that." His tone was wry. "I couldn't tell whether I was relieved or annoyed at your decision. I *did* know that I'd better get the hell out of that bed or all your good intentions would have gone flying."

She could have told him that he wasn't the only one to have suffered. She'd discovered in that moment that her unsullied virginal state existed merely because she'd never been sufficiently tempted before—not because she was strong-minded or disciplined or for any other reason. "It's a good thing that you didn't give me any longer to make up my mind," she admitted frankly.

"*Now* she tells me." Adam kept his voice light but there was a disturbing gleam in his eyes that showed how much her confession meant to him. "I think we'll have to do something about it. It's a pity that you obeyed orders and got dressed," he added, smoothing the hollow of her throat and letting his fingers drift down the neckline of her blouse to the soft valley below.

"It's just as well I did. You're entirely too good at pleading your cause." She quivered with delight under his caresses, then her own hands went up around his neck to smooth the crisp hair at the back of his head. "Considering the way things are between us, maybe it would be more discreet if I *did* go to St. Thomas for the rest of the time."

"I don't understand. Why in the devil should you go there?"

"Because I've never had an affair with anyone and even though I love you terribly, you'll have to give me time . . ." She broke off, frowning, as his shoulders started to shake with laughter.

Adam caught her close when she stiffened and would have stepped away. "You crazy little idiot! Stop struggling and listen to me. I love and adore you. And despite my lurid past, I have no intention of a tawdry little holiday affair with you. We're going to Government House and then to the cathedral this afternoon. If you'd bothered to read the card with those roses—"

At her delighted gasp, he loosened his clasp so that she could dart over to the bureau and open the tiny white envelope. An instant later, she was back, throwing her arms around him and standing on tiptoe to put her cheek against his. "You beast! Why didn't you say you wanted to marry me in the first place?"

"I didn't know I had to spell it out." He nuzzled the soft skin below her ear. "That's what happens when a man tries to be honorable."

"Oh, Adam!" She drew back with a stricken expression. "No wonder you looked so disillusioned when you came back."

"Well, finding you with your bags packed to take the next launch wasn't the reaction I was hoping for." His eyes darkened then as if the memory still rankled and he pulled her roughly against him. His head came down, covering her lips with a fierce demanding kiss that shattered every thought of resistance on Toni's part. Instinctively she responded, showing all the love that was in her heart as well as a need of her own.

Adam groaned and pulled her even closer, parting her lips as the kiss deepened—sending her senses spinning like a runaway carousel.

It was a long time before they returned to reality. When they did, he managed to say in uneven tones, "Fortunately, I'm a very forgiving man."

Toni's voice was soft and breathless as she rested her head against his chest, "So I've noticed."

He grinned. "And they were *very* expensive roses. There should be some compensation from one's nearest and dearest."

She nodded as if giving it serious thought. "You

have a point there," she agreed and stretched upward to brush her lips over the corner of his mouth in a butterfly caress. Naturally, Adam didn't let that go unchallenged and kissed her again.

"You were saying something about roses," Toni prompted him when they pulled reluctantly apart. It was difficult to remain coherent when all she really wanted was to stay close in Adam's arms and drown in those powerful kisses.

"I was?" Adam had trouble with his breathing, as well.

Toni's memory was coming back. "And compensation. But there isn't time."

"No?" His eyes were warm with teasing laughter.

"Not if the afternoon launch to St. Thomas leaves in twenty minutes." She looked at her watch. "Your note said we had an appointment at Government House for the license."

"Precisely." Adam's grin broadened as he pulled her back against him, letting her feel his strength. "But what I didn't put in the note was that I've hired a seaplane to fly us over and we don't have to leave for an hour yet."

Toni shivered again as she felt his hands move down her back to her hips and she whispered, "I suppose we'll have to fill all that time some way."

"Exactly what I was thinking." There was still laughter in his voice but there was a disturbing undertone, as well. "Maybe we could discuss island politics."

"Or track down a mattress for that other bed."

Adam's head came up then. "Is that necessary?"

She kept her tone solemn with an effort when she saw she had his full attention. "Not really. Especially since I'd just have to order another bucket of ice to go with it. The management would probably object because mattresses cost real money—Adam, darling—wait! We can't possibly . . ."

Her words were cut off suddenly as Adam swung her up in his arms and his mouth came down to cover hers.

It was an abrupt end to the discussion but there was compensation later.

Very nice compensation indeed!

About the Author

Glenna Finley is a native of Washington State. She earned her degree from Stanford University in Russian Studies and in Speech and Dramatic Arts, with emphasis on radio.

After a stint in radio and publicity work in Seattle, she went to New York City to work for NBC as a producer in its international division. In addition, she worked with the "March of Time" and *Life* magazine.

As a producer, she had her own show about activities in Manhattan, a show that was broadcast to England. The programs were similar to those of the "Voice of America."

Though her life in New York was exciting, she eventually returned to the Northwest where she married. Currently residing in Seattle with her husband, Donald Witte, and their son, she loves to travel, and draws heavily on her travels and experiences for the novels that have been published. Her books for NAL have sold several million copies.

O

More Romance from SIGNET

Buy them at your local

bookstore or use coupon

on next page for ordering.

⭕

Great Reading from SIGNET